Theophilus H. G. Puleston

The Story of a Quiet Country Parish

being gleanings of the history of Worthenbury, Flintshire

Theophilus H. G. Puleston

The Story of a Quiet Country Parish
being gleanings of the history of Worthenbury, Flintshire

ISBN/EAN: 9783337237523

Printed in Europe, USA, Canada, Australia, Japan

Cover: Foto ©Andreas Hilbeck / pixelio.de

More available books at **www.hansebooks.com**

THE STORY OF A QUIET COUNTRY PARISH.

BEING GLEANINGS OF THE

HISTORY OF WORTHENBURY,

FLINTSHIRE.

BY THE RECTOR, THE

REV. SIR T. H. GRESLEY PULESTON, BART.

London :

THE ROXBURGHE PRESS,

3, VICTORIA STREET,

WESTMINSTER.

TO THE

SACRED MEMORIES OF THE PAST.

PREFACE.

HAVING inherited some notes on the Parish of Worthenbury, which I only recently read, I determined, with these and other means within my reach, to write all that I could gather of the history of my parish, knowing, however, perfectly well, how imperfect my work must be, yet bearing in mind Machiavelli's saying that "it was better to do things badly than not to do them at all."

T. H. G. P.

The Story of a Quiet Country Parish,

BEING GLEANINGS OF

THE HISTORY OF WORTHENBURY, FLINTSHIRE.

———

Although Worthenbury does not appear to have been the scene of any great historical events, yet I hope to put together some gatherings which may have interest for those who know it and love it.

It is situated on the river Dee, is bounded on the south by Shropshire and on the north by Cheshire, and forms a part of the Hundred of Maelor, or Maelor Saesneg, to distinguish it from Maelor Cymraig in Denbighshire ; it is in the county of Flint, though separated from the main part of it by the portion of the county of Denbigh in the neighbourhood of Wrexham, through which one must pass for five or six miles before again touching Flintshire. The Hundred of Maelor Saesneg is about nine miles long by three and a half wide, and consists

of the Parishes of Bangor, Isycoed, Hanmer, Overton, part of Penley, part of Iscoed in the Parish of
Malpas and Worthenbury; also on the Welsh side
of the river Dee, of the Parish of Erbistock.

Pennant tells us there are several spots belonging
to this Hundred, insulated by Denbighshire, which
form nearly a connection between this and the
other part of the Hundred, and the chain is supposed
once to have been entire, but many of the links
were only fields which have now been lost to the
county. One of the Townships in the Parish of
Holt is known to have belonged to this Hundred—
Abenbury Fechan, a disjointed bit in the Parish of
Wrexham; Merford and Osley, in the Parish of
Gresford, were added by Henry VIII. to Flintshire,
and still form part of the county. If all the
missing links spoken of by Pennant could be found,
we should not be as much separated from our county
as we now are. It may be of interest to add here
that the name of Gresford, anciently Groesfordd, or
the Road of the Cross, is supposed to be derived
from an old cross, the shaft of which is still standing
within half a mile of the Church.

It is very difficult to form an opinion where the

first inhabitants of Britain came from, but Tacitus and Cæsar seem to have no doubt they came from Gaul. The country of Britain was divided into a number of small states, with a king over each, one of whom was chosen as a leader in the time of war; the people were considered brave and honest, easily provoked, but sincere and generous; they lived in huts of wattlework covered with clay; their food was flat cakes of bread, the flesh of animals killed in the chase, and milk. They were clothed with the skins of animals, which also formed the covering of the coracles in which they paddled along their rivers; their favourite beverage was metheglin, a fermented liquor made from honey, which is still used in some parts of Wales; bows and arrows with long spears were their implements of warfare, supplemented by chariots drawn by their ponies with scythes fixed on either side.

The priests and philosophers of the Britons were the Druids, by whom they were held in great veneration, not only for their learning but also because they were chosen from the most distinguished families. The word Druid is derived from the word Derw, meaning the oak, which they worshipped and held especially sacred when a sprig of mistletoe was found growing on it. The ancient Britons were idolators, and frequently sacrificed human beings to their gods. The remains of several of their temples are still to be seen in Anglesey and at Stonehenge, in Wiltshire, and wonderful works they are. When Julius Cæsar with his Roman army invaded Britain, 55 B.C., he found, as we may suppose, a very undisciplined but courageous force to oppose him, and we learn from him that the Britons had attained some civilisation, were much given to hospitality, and that they entertained their guests with the music of the harp, then, as now, the national instrument of Wales. The bards occupied an important position in the governing body of the nation; they were not only poets and minstrels, but also historians. Their object in life was said to be " to make manifest the truth and to diffuse the knowledge of it." One of the books which is supposed to date from their time is called the Triads. It was a traditional historic record, and on that account is most interesting. The people of this part of the country are descended from the ancient Britons, as for a long period they did not mix with the Saxons, and indeed, were for a long time at war with them, though no doubt in the process of time they did more or less intermarry with the Anglo-Saxon people.

When 'the Romans landed at or near Deal, the Britons fought so bravely that it was with the greatest difficulty that they effected a landing, and possibly they would have been driven away, but for the determined bravery of the Standard bearer of, I think, the 10th Legion, who jumped into the sea with his standard and called upon his comrades to defend it—it was the greatest disgrace to a Roman soldier to lose this or his shield, which the Roman mother, when strapping on her son, enjoined him either to return with it or on it.   Happily for us the Romans effected a landing and instructed our forefathers in all the arts of civilised Rome, during the time they remained on this Island ; for the Roman soldier then was not only a disciplined soldier but a skilful mechanic, as we may learn from Froude's " Life of Julius Cæsar," as well as from the splendid specimens that may now be seen among us of their work in Chester and other parts of England.   But especially are we indebted to the Romans for their exertions in trying to bring us to the knowledge of our Saviour. In A.D. 180, Lucius, a king of Britain, was by the preaching of one of the Christian Fathers converted to the faith. He is said to have founded the monastery of Bangor as a seat of learning, or at all events to have done all that he could for the good cause. An Emperor of Rome, Constantine Clor, married Princess Helena, a Briton, and their son, Constantine the Great, was the first Christian Emperor. He too furthered the work, and so from a very early date Christianity flourished in Britain, though it was from a still earlier period established in Wales. The Romans left Britain, A.D. 448, as their troops were wanted at home. Then the Britons having no longer the disciplined legions of Rome to help them to resist the incursions of their troublesome neighbours, the Picts and Scots, sought help from the Saxons who were so pleased with Britain that they determined to conquer it for themselves, which they ultimately did ; thus in a very short time, the laws, language, and people, were changed on this Island ; and after the defeat of Caractacus the Britons were little better than slaves. Cadwallader was the last of the British race who enjoyed the title of King of

Britain, though the Cambrians set up a new Government for themselves after his death; but their rulers were called Princes of Wales, and with these Cambrians rested the remains of the British nation.

In ancient time the rivers Severn and Dee separated Wales from England; but as a protection in the perpetual border frays, Offa, King of Mercia, made a dyke, which was probably in his time the real boundary between England and Wales, and to this day the Welsh language generally prevails on the Cambrian side of it, while it is seldom spoken by the dwellers on the English side. This dyke extended, it is said, from Prestatyn on the Dee to a little below Bristol.

The earliest notice known of the Hundred of Maelor is about the middle of the 6th century—Bangor Monastery was then flourishing, though there were at that time perpetual conflicts between the Saxons, who were trying to win, and the Britons who were striving to save their country. About 540 A.D., Cunetha Whedig succeeded in right of his mother to the sovereignty of Cambria, afterwards his sons and grandsons sub-divided the country among them, giving their own names to them; one of them was named Maelor and he was master of the two Maelors, Saesneg and Cymraig. At that time the Britons too had a considerable portion of the country on the east side of the river Dee. About 567, Cunetha Whedig is said to have founded Oswestry, which was then called Llundain or Little London, until Oswald, King of Northumberland, built a cross there, which was said to be the first erected in England, which caused its name to be changed to Crossoswalt which soon became Oswestry.

Early in the 9th century, King Egbert, who united the seven kingdoms of the Saxons and became first sole monarch of England, won the city of Chester from the Welsh—a most valuable acquisition, as it is the key to North Wales, as the land adjoining it is a flat country. He seems not to have interfered with Maelor Saesneg because he had a Danish invasion to occupy his attention. In 887 we have again a notice of the Hundred of Maelor as Roderic the Great apportioned it to his third son Merfyn as a part of Powys land, Maelor Cymraig in Denbighshire and Maelor Saesneg in Flintshire, being a part of his inheritance. In after times this country was conquered by Harold for Edward the Confessor, whose son Athelstan laid the Welsh Princes under tribute. Their downfall as a nation may be dated from this and their territory was gradually diminished. William the Conqueror, however, did not dispossess the Welsh of Flintshire although it was under his rule, and he joined nearly the whole of the county to the Palatinate of Chester. In Domesday Book we find the whole of this country running from the estuary of the Dee is surveyed for the Conqueror under the name of Atiscross, and Maelor Saesneg is included in a Hundred called Dudestan.

In spite of the heroic deeds of Llewelyn ap Gruffydd, the last Welsh Prince, the English power over Wales increased, and he was glad to conclude a treaty with Henry III. of England by which he was to retain the sovereignty of North Wales and Powys land, on payment of a large tribute ; this arrangement, however, did not last long, and in 1282, after the overthrow of Llewelyn, the sovereignty of Wales was extinguished, and Edward I. by a statute made at Ruthlan, incorporated it with the crown of England.

It was Edward I. who divided England into

counties. It seems strange that the king should
not have enacted that Maelor Saesneg should
continue according to Domesday survey, but ignor-
ing the natural boundary which the Dee here
presents, as the limit of the Principality, he restores
it to Wales, and apportions it to the newly formed
county of Flint. A story connecting English Maelor
with the reign of Edward I. given at length by
Powel and quoted by Nicholas, author of " Annals
and Antiquities of Wales," has a special connection
with my present purpose: "The Lord of Dînas
Brân at this time was Gruffydh ap Madawe,
Lord of Bromfield, who had made himself very
obnoxious to his countrymen by his treachery in
forsaking his native prince and siding with Henry
III. and Edward I. This man died about 1270,
leaving a widow, Emma, daughter of James, Lord
Audley, and four sons, Madawe, Llewelyn, Gruffydh,
and Owen. The king gave the wardship of Madawe,
who had for his portion Bromfield and Yale, the
castle of Dînas Brân with the reversion of Maelor
Saesneg," corresponding with Emral Flintshire,
" the other side of the Dee from Wrexham Parish,
while Maelor Cymraig was in that parish, after his

mother's death, to John, Earl of Warren ; and granted the wardship of Llewelyn, to whose part Chirk and Manhendwy came, to Roger Mortimer, a grandson of Lord Mortimer, of Wigmore." These guardians so guarded their wards that they never returned to their possessions. Pennant, quoting from the " Bodleian," says they were drowned under Holt Bridge ; and Yorke, in the " Royal Tribes," says, " As it might happen, the wards were missed and were no more found." Then the guardians obtained the lands for themselves by charters from the king.

Powel's account of the widow's dowry and subsequent disposition of it, involves quite a different question. After stating the guardianship of the sons as above, it says that Gruffydh's wife, having in her possession for her dowry Maelor Saesneg, Hopesdale and Moulsdale, with the presentation of Bangor Rectory, and seeing her sons disinherited and done away, the fourth dead without issue, and doubting lest Gruffydh, her only remaining child, should not continue long, conveyed the estate to her own kin, the Audleys, and from them it went to the house of Derby, who in after years sold some of it to Sir John

Glynne, Sergeant-at-law. The Salusbury pedigree book belonging to Sir W. W. Wynn says, " Emma, daughter of Henry de Audley, as appears by the inquisition taken 13th July, 1277, had for her jointure Maelor Saesneg because she was an Englishwoman, and her house of Emrall was built for her." How long Emma Audley was in possession of Emrall Hall is uncertain, but it appears by an inquisition of 5 Edward I. that she was then dispossessed of all lands in both Maelors, and died at Overton in 1278, possibly in the old castle. The memory of Edward I.'s queen being hurried to Carnarvon Castle for her accouchement is still preserved in this parish by the Queen's Ford over the river Elf, and at Overton by the Queen's Bridge. Her son was created Prince of Wales and Earl of Chester.

In 1279 Richard de Pyvelesdon restores to the king all his lands and tenements in Worthenbury, having probably only held them for·two years, or possibly five, as there is a deed, 1284, speaking of the " foresta domini Rogeri de Pyvelesdon " at Willington. There seem to have been two parties at work, one trying to get Emrall and the property attached to it for Richard, the other for Roger Puleston, but in the end Roger Puleston, the king's trusted friend and servant, gets it.

As the Puleston family figure a great deal in the history of this parish, it will be well to tell something of their antecedents. They were an old Shropshire family with possessions in Staffordshire. They owned the manor of Pillesdon, and took their name from it, as was then the custom. Eudo de Pillesdon was living in 15 Henry II. Two of them were crusaders. Warrenis de Pillesden died on his way to Jerusalem in the time of Richard II. Jordan de Pillesdon had letters of protection from Henry III. on going to the Holy Land. The name of Pyllesdon frequently occurs in connection with those of Audley and L'Estrange, and it may have been owing to a friendship with the Audleys that de Pyllesdon was chosen to succeed Emma at Emrall.

In the Salusbury book Puleston and Hanmer are mentioned as settlers in Maelor; probably all the other inhabitants were of British descent. In numberless old deeds and charters there is frequent mention of the de Pulesdons, who were in the reign of Edward I. warm partisans of the king. The Roger

mentioned as owning a forest near Willington was
the first Sir Roger who was called of Emral, and
he was established there about 1282 ; he was in high
favour with the king, who granted it to him.
Unfortunately, the original grant is lost, so that the
exact date is not known.   The earls of Derby we
know retained a good deal of the gift which I have
mentioned as made to them by Emma Audley, the
presentation to Bangor Rectory, which included for
about 300 years the chapel at Emral with the cure of
souls attached.

The influence of the English knights (Pulesdons
and Hanmers) seems in a great measure to have
affected the nationality of this part of the Hundred
of Maelor ; probably before their coming the
inhabitants were all Welsh, as to this day most of
the fields bear Welsh names ; but from this date the
language, manners, and customs of the inhabitants
are exactly like those of England, and so, too, for
the most part are the names.   The influx of Emma
Audley, who had a sort of Regal State, and an
English knight of good standing at the court of
England with his followers, must have aided greatly
the prosperity and probably the civilisation of

Worthenbury and the surrounding district, and it would be of the greatest possible interest to know more of the inner life of these people, though I have no clue to it.

Edward I. did not take the eastern side of the river Dee in the Hundred of Maelor from Wales, and from his day to the time of Henry VIII. it was unchanged. That monarch, however, seems to have had a great desire to straighten his boundary lines for the purpose of improving the local government of his kingdom. In 1583 a statute was passed "concerning the laws to be used in Wales," by which was enacted that Oswestry, Whittington, Ellesmere, and various adjacent parts should henceforth be annexed to the County of Salop; but he joined Hope and some portion of the south-eastern part of the county to this Hundred, and made it what it now is except in an ecclesiastical sense, as in 1849, soon after I became Rector of Worthenbury, the parishes of Bangor, Overton, Hanmer-with-Bronnington, Threapwood, and Worthenbury were transferred by an Order in Council from the Diocese of Chester to that of St. Asaph.

But to go back. 20th March, 12 Edward I., by

letters patent at Rhuddlan, he grants the office of Viscount of Carnarvon to Richard Puleston during his pleasure and makes the same grant to Roger as to Anglesey. This Richard seems to have been the original Puleston grantee of Emral and that it was he who restored it to the king in 1279, who then granted it to Roger Puleston, his personal friend and favourite. The exact date as I have said is unknown, but he is described as of " Embers Hall," 1283 : in 1284 he is appointed Sheriff of Anglesey and Constable of Carnarvon Castle ; he married Agnes, a daughter of David le Clerk, Baron of Malpas, and died in 1294. The story is told by Caradoc, of Llancaroun, in his history of Wales, how he met his death. " King Edward was now in actual enmity and war with the King of France, for the carrying on of which he wanted a liberal subsidy and supply from his subjects." With a great deal of passion and reluctancy " a tax was levied in various places of his kingdom and ' especially in Wales.' The Welsh ' never being acquainted with such large contributions before,' violently stormed and exclaimed against it ; but not satisfied with storming and vilifying they took their own captain, Roger de Pulesdon, who was appointed collector of the said subsidy, and hanged him together with divers others who abetted the collecting of the tax." He then tells that "the king being acquainted with these insurrections and desirous to quell the stubbornness of the Welsh, but most of all to revenge the death of his great favourite Roger de Pulesdon, recalled his brother Edmund, Earl of Lancaster," etc. The collection of this tax commenced in 1293, and Pulesdon's murder must have taken place after 18th January, 1294, for on that day he witnessed at Emral (being then a Knight) a deed to which Richard de Pulesdon is a party.

In the second volume of his tours in Wales, Pennant says there is at Carnarvon a very ancient house called Plas Pulesdon, which is remarkable for the fate of its first owner, etc. The representative in Parliament is chosen by the Burgesses of Conwy, Pwllheli, Carnarvon, etc. The first member they elected was John Puleston, the second time they sent a representative was 1st of Edward VI. when Robert Puleston was chosen, while the county elected John Puleston ; it seems as if both Borough and County tried in this way to make reparation to the family for the cruelty practised on their ancestor.

3

As this "veritable history" is written for the
dwellers in the Hundred of Maelor, it may be of
interest to tell the several derivations of this name.
One is that it is from the word Maelawr or Market,
and Dr. Owen Pugh says there are several districts
so called in the marshes of Wales, and these were
neutral ground in the time of war, because trade was
carried on there. This in a manner might apply
to this part of the Hundred of Maelor, as there were
in this parish two corn mills, and closely adjoining
a fulling mill and some salt works. To our modern
ideas it seems difficult to imagine how all this trade
put together can have been of much importance—
though the smallness of the population and the
simple habits of the period would not demand a
great deal. It seems, however, there is little doubt
that several Frankish settlers came into this Hundred
in very early days.

In Domesday Book, 1086, Hurdingberie had three
Franks settled in the manor, pioneers, no doubt, in
the cloth trade, afterwards the greatest trade in
England; and near Overton to this day there is a
farm called Carrego Francod, while on the Ellesmere
side there are English and Welsh Frankton. The

fulling mill previously referred to is supposed to have been the present Corn Mill at Halghton; while the two corn mills mentioned in the minister's accounts of Edward IV. have long been pulled down. One of these stood near Emral Hall, which was pulled down in memory of men I have known, the other is said to have been at this end of Emral Park, but when that was pulled down is altogether unknown. In the Parish Registers of Hanmer of the earliest date there are names of people who were evidently attracted there by the cloth trade: Roger and Bartholomew Keay came from Yorkshire; Roger Gott is married in 1563. There were also a family of dyers by name Roan. Richard Ridgway, too, comes from Cheshire to the Pandy in Halghton; all this to some extent supports this origin of the name Maelor. But other writers suppose that the name came from Cunetha Weldig, one of the Holy Families of the Isle of Britain, who is said to have been the first who bestowed land on the Church in Britain; he died A.D. 389.

At the present day English Maelor has not advanced in commercial importance, indeed, I am afraid, if it ever possessed any, it has lost it.

This country owes a great deal to the Romans, as they opened it out by the magnificent roads they made through it. We all know what railroads have done for England in our day; but the improvement must have been even greater in the days of the Romans. Throughout the length and breadth of this country, roads were made and cities founded by them which still bear marks of their authors. Some of these roads and cities retain the names given them by their founders. Between the cities, stations and camps were established. and these were connected by broad and skilfully formed roads, some of which still exist, and are models of what a main road ought to be: some are lost by diversion of traffic: but still names which are familiar to us all, remind us of the Romans when they occupied Britain. Our own parish and neighbourhood are very much identified with some of them, as the Romans had a camp on the east side of Emral Park, probably to protect the station at Bangor Iscoyd, which lay between their cities of Uricanium and Deva, or Chester. In an old book called "Iter Britannicum" there is a place mentioned called Bonium, Borium, or Boium: this was supposed to be where the village of Bangor now stands. This is believed to be the Banchorium of Richard of Cirencester. From the institution of the first Christian college here, it is said to have derived its name of Ban-Gór, which the Saxons changed into Banclurna Byrig, a name descriptive of its importance as a privileged town. Owen Pughe says, " Bangor is the same as college in Welsh—a society of this sort being called Cór, from the Latin word *chori*, to which the word Ban, signifying superior, was subsequently prefixed; it has also been called Bangor Maelor, Bangor Monachorum, or, as now, Bangor Isycoed, or Bangor-under-the-Wood."

There are many remains of Roman stations in Hanmer Parish; one of the best known of these is the mound with a few Scotch firs growing on it, up to the Whitchurch and Wrexham road. The mound is circular and trenched round; it is considered by antiquarians to be of British origin, though adopted by the Romans as a camp.

Some years ago, Canon Lee says, the occupier of Eglwys-y-groes Farm, in digging for sand, brought to light a jar of coins, most of them bearing the name of the Emperor Constantine, A.D. 306, while others were of an older date. This emperor was born in Britain, and his mother was the pious Empress Helena, a daughter of a British prince.

The story of Constantine's conversion to the Christian faith is well known ; in consequence of a vision of a flaming cross with the inscription, *in hoc signo vinces* (under this sign thou shalt conquer), his standard displayed a cross. He showed great favour to Christians, and encouraged the building of churches. The story goes that Helena found a piece of the true cross at Jerusalem, which through a native prince came into the possession of Edward I. when he conquered Wales, who deposited it at Westminster Abbey; this gives an especial interest to these coins bearing Constantine's name.

There is another circular mound below the village of Hanmer, and near Willington Cross is to be seen a square camp. A Roman road undoubtedly passed through this district; the route given from Wroxeter is by Grinshill, by Broughton, near Sansaw, through Loppington to Bettisfield. Mr. Lee said between Northwood and Bettisfield the road branched off, one going by Hampton, Penley, and Rhyd y Cyffin to Bangor, probably going through a part of

Worthenbury Parish by Adravalyn. He said there were in his time some who remembered a pavement on this road, called a Roman pavement. The other branch road went by the Three Fingers to Talarn Green, and on to Chester by the vale of the Dee. Another branch went by Eglwys Cross, then past the Yew Tree Farm to the old Hall, crossing the Chester road just mentioned by Willington Cross, and so on by Calika Farm through Mulsford and Emral, through Billington's Farm, where a permanent road has just been discovered to Bangor.

The word " Street" when it is applied to a country road as in Street Issa and Street Luddon and in Watling Street, always denotes a Roman road. Watling Street just mentioned was one of the most important of the Roman roads leading from London through the midland counties (in both of which it is still called by this name) to this country. This road was originally thrown up to a considerable height above the level, no doubt to keep it firm and dry. The sides were kept up by staves, and lesser wood was woven in between, hence the name of Watling as the Saxons called these wattles. The old British name of this road was Sarn Guetheling or Irish

Road ; Sarn, meaning a road or causeway is still in use in this parish and other places in this neighbourhood.

I have already told that Roger Puleston had a wood at Gwillington, which in the attestation is called Willington, so that we see the letters W and G were used as the same letter 600 years ago, and in the reign of Henry VIII. this parish is called Worthembre and Guothumbre. Before the Roman Invasion of Britain, the Druids had near us many places where they celebrated their religious rites : one of these was said to be on a mound at Iscoed, which I saw opened, but alas, nothing of interest was found. There was the Gelli or Grove which those Druid's affected, and it certainly is interesting to think of these places as connected with those mysterious people and their idolatrous worship " of strange gods."

One relic of those far off times we have yet among us on the river Dee—in the coracle, though it has now lost its right to the name as it is covered with pitched canvas, instead of a hide. We who see it constantly in the salmon fishing season scarcely notice it, but it is striking to a stranger and especially when he has read Julius Cæsar's account of Britain in his day ; and it was before Christ was born that the Romans came first to this Island and while they yet ruled Britain, that He was crucified, and tradition says that St. Paul, Joseph of Arimathea, or one of the Apostles brought the good tidings of great joy to this Island. It seems, however, more probable that Bryan, the father of Caractacus, who was taken prisoner to Rome and there converted to the faith and on being released returned to his native land, was the means of bringing Christianity to Britain. It is also said that Claudia, who is spoken of together with Pudens by St. Paul, was a British lady, because a British lady of that name is known to have been a wife of Pudens.

The story of Joseph of Arimathea coming to Britain with eleven companions seems to rest a good deal on tradition ; he is said to have been driven from Jerusalem by the Jews because he begged the body of Christ from Pilate, and to have brought with him some of the Saviour's blood which he washed from the wound in His side, and that when he arrived in Britain he founded the Abbey of Glaston-bury. The church which he and his companions built there, is believed to have been of wickerwork, and to have been dedicated to Mary, the mother of our Lord.

William of Malmesbury, who lived soon after the Norman conquest, says there are documents of no small credit which say that " no other hands than those of the Apostles of Christ erected the Church at Glastonbury," while Gildas, the most ancient of our historians, says the Church of Christ was planted in Britain in the last year of Tiberius, in whose reign Christ was crucified.

There can be no doubt that Britain came early into Christ's vineyard, for Tertullian writing A.D. 209, speaks of British Christians, and in the next century British Bishops are spoken of as attending Councils of the Church.

The writer of " Vale Royal " says, " the Christian faith and baptism " came into Chester in the reign of Lucius, a king of the Britons, probably from Cambria, A.D. 140.

When the Roman roads were being made across the Hundred of Maelor, the first germs of Christianity were coming to life, which rapidly drove away the superstitions of the Druids and the idolatry of the natives. To Bangor Iscoyd belongs the honour of being the site of one of the earliest Christian seminaries in Britain, and as such has deservedly a great interest for every Welshman. We read of Lucius, King of Britain, greatly furthering the work of converting his subjects to the Christian faith, by sending some of his learned men to the Bishop of Rome to receive instruction; they brought back this remarkable letter, " You have received in the Kingdom of Britain, by God's mercy, both the law and the faith of Christ. You have both the Old and the New Testament. Out of the same, through God's grace by the advice of your realm, take the law, and by the same, through God's sufferance, rule your Kingdom of Britain, for in that kingdom you are God's vicar." 1335236

The king wisely acted on this advice, and feeling the responsibility which rested on him, he did his utmost to oppose the worship of idols, and to have his people instructed in the principles of the Gospel, and for this purpose founded Bangor as a seminary of learning; and the venerable Bede, writing in A.D. 733, speaks of it as flourishing in the time of Augustine till Ethelfrid, king of the Angles, in his wars with the Britons in the beginning of the 7th century, slew about 1,200 of the monks who were present, though at a distance, on the field of battle where their fellow countrymen were soon to be engaged in battle with the Angles, and they were praying to the Almighty for the Britons' success against the Saxons.

The " Venerable " Bede, a man of eminent piety and great learning, is the first writer who gives us any information about Bangor, and as he was a Saxon, his writings were not friendly to the Britons; but his character stands high as an authority, so that no one would impute to him a wilful misstatement; he died in 735. This would show that he was alive about a century after the destruction of the monastery at Bangor. His account is this of the slaughter of these monks : " Ethelfrid, the most powerful king of the Angles, having raised a mighty army, made a terrible slaughter of the perfidious nation of the Britons. When he was ready to engage, he saw the priests who were assembled to pray to God for the success of their army, standing at a distance out of danger, whereupon he asked who those men were, and to what intent they were brought together to that place? King Ethelfrid having been told that they were monks from Bangor, who were come to pray for the success of his enemies, said, ' If it be so that they cry to their gods against us, they do truly fight against us, though they have no weapons, since they oppose us by their imprecations,' whereupon he gave orders to attack them first, which was done, and after their slaughter he destroyed all the forces of the perfidious Britons, though with considerable loss."

It is said that only fifty of the monks escaped by flight, and that Brochel, their head, fled at once, leaving his brethren to their cruel fate. After this massacre the monastery fell into decay, and William of Malmesbury writes of it, "There then remained only the footsteps of so great a place, so many ruinous churches and such heaps of rubbish as were hardly elsewhere to be met with." Speed, who was born at Malpas, 1552, says Bangor is the first monastery that is read of in the world, and it is said there were 2,400 monks there, who in turn, a 100 at a time, read prayers and sang hymns continuously. Probably the number of these monks, as well as those slaughtered is greatly exaggerated, as well as the character of the buildings which were erected there, as the probability is that they were mainly like other churches of that early date, of wattle and daub, with such stone as could be readily procured for foundations. A great many of the monks devoted themselves to the education of those who came under their care, while others wholly occupied their time in the cultivation of their fields for their common support.

That Bangor was a place of learning is beyond doubt—just like one of our modern universities ; but it is by no means safe to place too great a reliance on the records we have of those far off times. There were, moreover, three Bangors, one in Ireland, the other in Carnarvonshire, and our neighbouring one, all founded by St. Deiniol, who is the patron saint of Worthenbury Church, which is an offshoot from Bangor. At the time of which I am writing, England was under the rule of its Saxon conquerors ; the Britons, instead of submitting, retired to their mountains, and, led by their Cambrian princes, kept up a continual warfare against the Anglo-Saxons, who had established a sevenfold government called the Heptarchy. The Britons clung to the religion of Christ, but Southey says for 150 years Christ disappeared from the Heptarchy, and the country was in pagan darkness.

At this time Pope Gregory, surnamed the Great, went to inspect some foreign merchandise in the market at Rome, and among other things exposed for sale, were some fair haired boys of great beauty; he asked to what country they belonged, and was told they were Angles from Deira, and with a pun on both words, said they would be angels if they were saved (De irâ) from the anger of God by becoming Christians. It was he who sent Augustine to this island, who found to his astonishment that the people of Cambria and Cornwall were not in the neglected state he expected to find them, for there were in those parts seven Bishops and one Archbishop "most religious Prelates and Abbots living by the labour of their hands." St. Augustine tried to bring these rulers of the Anglican church into conformity with Rome, but the British Prelates declined to submit to the supremacy of the Pope, and a great council was convened at which seven Bishops and many learned men from the monastery of Bangor, with Demetrius their head, were present.

The controversy was said to have been very warm; but Augustine's persuasions and threats were of no avail, for the British clergy would not submit to him or consent to adopt the Romish teaching as to baptism "according to the rites he wished to intro-duce." "They had received the doctrine and discipline of their church from the Apostles of Christ, and would not change for any man's pleasure." We are told that Augustine, mortified at his want of success with these British Prelates, denounced against their church the judgment of God, predicting that as they would not have peace with their Christian brethren, they would soon have war with their Pagan enemies, and because they would not aid him in his intended conversion of the Saxons, they would find speedy death by the swords of those to whom they had refused to preach the Word of Life.

Reynolds reports a second meeting, and states that before it took place the Britons consulted a holy man as to whether they should submit to Augustine or not. The advice they received was to take the course he showed them and to follow the same : " if he be a man of God, this they would discern by seeing if he was meek and humble of heart, but they might be sure, if he is stout and· proud, he is not of God." Their adviser counsels them to let Augustine and his company arrive first at their place of meeting, and if he rises and receives them with welcome and reverence they were to be encouraged to take confidence in him. On this advice they acted. Augustine entered the place first with great pomp, and when the Bishops of the British Church came in, he did not move to salute them. " This, they taking very ill in everything, exhorted one another not to yield a jot unto him by any means, for, say they, he will not deign so much as to rise out of his chair to salute us ; how much more when we have submitted to his jurisdiction will he despise us and set us at nought." We are then told that after this Austin complained to king Ethelbert, who marched against them, met them at Chester, where the Britons received a great overthrow.

The foregoing account shows a strong bias in favour of the British Church, but putting all prejudice on one side, we, who have for many long ages enjoyed the goodly heritage of a church with a pure and simple ritual and faith, cannot but look back with satisfaction at the conduct of these rulers of our mother church whose teaching was as Reynolds says, free from what he calls Popish wiles. Transubstantiation was then not thought of, Papal indulgences were unknown, the celibacy of the Clergy was not enforced, and as far as we know, it was a Scriptural creed which our forefathers were taught by the monks of Bangor 1300 years ago, and which we should value and cling to. I ought to add that Augustine, who prophesied evil to the monks of Bangor, died five years before their destruction by the Saxons, so that he could not possibly have instigated this cruelty. To more modern writers we are indebted for a fuller and more graphic account of the fall of Bangor.

The following particulars are collected from " The Vale Royal," Powel's " History of Wales " and Lewis's " Topographical Dictionary of Wales " :—

Ethelfrid, king of North Northumberland, had been very successful in extending his dominions. The Britons who dwelt in Chester provoked him to war, whereupon he assembled an army and laid siege to the town. The citizens, trusting to their numbers, marched out to meet him with all their forces to give him battle. They were attended by a large body of monks from Bangor ; these were under the protection of Brockwall, Prince of Powys, and stood at a short distance to encourage their friends by their prayers and exhortations.   It was then that the slaughter already mentioned took place.   The Britons, disheartened by the slaughter of the priests, received a total defeat, and Chester was compelled to surrender. After the battle, Ethelfrid marched to Bangor and utterly destroyed that ancient seat of learning, and burnt their valuable library.   Bede speaks most bitterly of Brockwall's conduct in leaving the unprotected monks to the fury of the Saxons.   If he deserves this, he seems to have made a noble effort to retrieve his fault by hastening to Bangor, and though too late to stay the destroying hand of Ethelfrid, he collected such troops as he could and successfully opposed the passage of the Dee, which the Saxon king attempted to cross with a view of making further inroads into British territory, aided by Cadwan, king of North Wales, and Meredydd, king of South Wales, and these, Dunawd, abbot of Bangor, joined, who was one of the fifty who escaped from the massacre at Chester.   He delivered an oration to the army, and concluded by ordering the soldiers to kiss the ground in commemoration of the body of Christ, and to take up water in their hands out of the river Dee and drink it in remembrance of His sacred blood.

This seems to have inspired these men with courage, and they met the Saxons so bravely that Ethelfrid was completely defeated, himself dangerously wounded, and more than a thousand of his army killed and the rest put to flight ; and thus the one great battle in English Maelor, and probably not more than three miles from the table on which I am writing, ended in a complete victory for the British people. When Edelfrid marched to Bangor after the battle of Chester it is not known on which side the river Dee he went. If by the eastern bank, and he crossed the Dee at Holt, then Mr. Thomas is probably correct in thinking that the slaughter of the monks took place at Pantyrochain (dingle of mourning), though it seems more probable that he would avoid crossing the Dee and pass along the eastern side, or why should the Cambrian princes be so eager to oppose him ? If this was so, the massacre might have taken place in the field assigned it by the indefatigable Canon Lee, called Maes-gr-ing (field of agony), which he said was near Worthenbury.

However this may have been, it must have been but a poor consolation to the few survivors to see the Saxons defeated, as this would not restore them to their homes or give them back those whom they had loved and lost. Sadly and mournfully must the Abbot and his few remaining brethren have looked their last farewell on their beloved monastery, and thought of past happy and useful days, gone by for ever. No more would the sound of prayer and praise be heard within those blackened walls. Truly the glory of Bangor was departed, and "their house was left unto them desolate." No restoration was ever attempted, so time finished what the destroying hand of the Saxon began, but so large must have been the monastery that "five centuries afterwards there were many remains of churches and ruins." Probably the truth is that none of the buildings there were of a permanent character, such as Vale of Cucis Abbey, near Llangollen, but dwellings of wattle and daub, and the Hengwert MS. of Mr. Vaughan, who was born in 1592, in some measure bears out this. He says the town and monastery had so felt the injuries of time that hardly any remains of the ruins were left, and he only found the rubbish of the two principal gates, Porth Klais and Porth Wyan, the former looking towards England, the latter towards Wales. They were about a mile apart, with the Dee running between them.

This gives us some idea of the extent of the city which lay between these gates.

Leland, who travelled through this country in the reign of Henry VIII., writes : " The next parish down the Dee is Bangor," this is the paroche where the great abbey was ; "that is as much as lieth beyond Dee on the north side is in Welsh Maelor, and that is half the parish, but the abbey stood in English Maelor on the south of Dee, and it is ploughed ground now, where the abbey stood, by the space of a good Welsh mile. They ploughed up bones of the monks and pieces of their bones and sepulchres. The abbey stood in a fair Dee valley and Dee ran by it. The compass of it was as a walled town, and ' yet remaineth the name of a gate called Porth Hogan by north, and the name of the other Porth Clays by south ' (probably near where Cloy Hall now stands). Dee seems changing its bottom, runneth now through the middle of these gates, one a mile from the other ; and in this ground be ploughed up foundations of squared stones, and Roman money is found there." This shows that there had previously been a Roman camp where the abbey was afterwards placed.

Canon Lee says the third gate to the abbey was Dwyn-gre, no doubt the Dungray, which lies between Worthenbury and Bangor. Pennant, writing of the abbey and its precincts, says it must have been large, for the monks maintained themselves by the labour of their own hands; the simple and unlearned pro· vided meat and clothing for the learned. He says he could discover no remains of this famous place, and found nothing of higher antiquity than four stone coffin lids and an old stone cross, all dug up in the churchyard. Even these remains have now disappeared.

The Hanmer notes say : " There is at Marchwiel part of an old cross found on the further bank of the large meadow to the south-west of Bangor, and about two furlongs above the church. A higher flood than usual had made a breach and exposed it."

It consists of a large square pedestal and the cross with the dexter limb broken off; the shaft is about nine feet high. There were also found a quantity of black oak beams. This field is still called Maes y groes—field of the cross. These relics were found in 1849.

When the present rectory was built, 1868-9, the stone sill of a large window was found in digging the foundations, also a curious sort of stone box. In the College library of St. David's there is a MS., which tradition says was brought from Bangor by one of the monks flying for his life; it is said to be marked with dark spots, which, on being analysed, are found to be blood. More than 1,200 years have passed since these events took place, so that it is little wonder that there are few remains of this famous monastery. Let us earnestly hope that the fruits of this early Apostolic teaching may never be wholly lost, and let us ever think with reverence of these holy men who were pioneers in the work of founding Christ's Church in Britain, for we must not forget that the British Church was flourishing when Augustine came here as a missionary from Rome. It is said that the surviving monks of

Bangor sought refuge at Bangor in Carnarvonshire ; others are said to have floated down the Dee to Chester and crossed thence to Ireland, and founded a monastery of the same name in the county Down.

The following lines by Sir Walter Scott, written in 1817, seem to be an appropriate ending to all that I have been able to gather of the history of Bangor Monastery. The tune to which these verses is adapted is called the Monks' March, and is supposed to have been played at their disastrous procession when they went to pray for the success of their countrymen against the Saxons.

When the heathen trumpets' clang
Round beleagured Chester rang,
Veiled nun and friar gray
Marched from Bangor's fair abbaye ;
High their holy anthem sounds,
Cestrias Vale the hymn rebounds,
Floating down the Sylvan Dee—
    O miserere Domine !

On the long procession goes,
Glory round their crosses glows,
And the Virgin mother mild
In their peaceful banner smiled ;
Who could think such saintly band
Doomed to feel unhallowed hand ?
Such was the Divine decree—
    O miserere Domine !

Bands that masses only sang,
Hands that censers only swang,
Met the northern bow and bill,
Heard the war cry wild and shrill ;
Woe to Brockmael's feeble hand,
Woe to Oldfrid's bloody brand,
Woe to Saxon cruelty—
                    O miserere Domine !

Weltering amid warriors slain,
Spurned by steeds with bloody mane,
Slaughtered down by Heathen blade
Bangor's peaceful monks are laid ;
Words of parting rest unspoke,
Mass unsang and bread unbroke,
For their souls for charity
                    Sing *O miserere Domine !*

Bangor ! o'er the murder wail !
Long thy ruins told the tale ;
Shattered towers and broken arch
Long recalled the woeful march.
On thy shrines no tapers burn;
Never shall thy priests return,
The Pilgrim sighs and sings for thee—
                    O miserere Domine !

There is proof of the missionary work the monastery did in the names of abbeys which have sprung from Bangor, but as far as I know there is no proof that they tried to convert their Saxon neighbours, and it may be, that it was because they neglected this obvious duty, that God allowed them to fall by the swords of the Saxons as Augustine predicted.

In those early days of our Church, religious teaching was for the most part confined to the preaching of monks sent out from monasteries, or Cathedral Churches; generally at some cross erected by the side of one of the great roads, where from time to time a congregation would meet one of these itinerant instructors. The names of several of these crosses still linger in this neighbourhood, though I know of none in this parish unless the Holy Bush was used for this purpose; there were, however, two in Bangor.

Tradition says that at first the spiritual needs of Worthenbury were supplied by the monks of Bangor, and in after days certainly the care of souls of the dwellers in and around Emral was under the charge of Bangor.

Hanmer Parish is especially rich in names calling to mind the early years of our church. Traws-tre-Croxton. Eglwys y groes, all names derived from cross, though the last named means more "the Church of the Cross," and is supposed to have been the site of the oldest British Church in this neighbourhood, though there is little doubt that in still older days it had been used by the Druids and afterwards occupied by the Romans as a station, in whose time this church may have been built. Croxton is supposed to be the land assigned as an endowment for this church. But the most interesting memorial of the British Church there, is Llyn Bedydd, a lake of baptism. The custom was in those days to baptise in rivers and fountains, though afterwards, in consequence of persecutions, fonts were erected in private houses, and when persecution died away, in the church porch, afterwards in the church itself; but in the days I am writing about, there were very few churches, and a cross, an appropriate reminder of the blessings promised by Christ's death, was the place of meeting: then as time went on, oratories and chapels were built, so that in bad weather services might be conducted in them all the year round.

As soon as the inhabitants of a district were converted to the Christian faith, a church was built by the owners of the land for the accommodation of their tenants and labourers, and the limits of the estate became the boundary of the parish. In the middle of the 7th century the divisions of parishes became more defined, though for a long period all churches and chapelries were considered dependent on the mother church, which was the name given to the cathedral or the great church of the district, to which was reserved all rights of burial and baptism. Eventually the parish churches had fixed ministers, and the tithe of the parish was appropriated for the spiritual work in the church of that parish, which in turn became the mother church of any chapel or oratory built by a landowner near his mansion for his own convenience.

This is the way that Worthenbury was in some measure dependent on Bangor; it is evidently a relationship going back to a very ancient date. Worthenbury has probably been closely connected with Bangor Monastery from the foundation of the abbey; it is on this account that I have entered so fully into the history of Bangor in this book, as in writing of Bangor at that date I am in fact writing of Worthenbury. It was moreover to the influence of Deiniol, the celebrated son of the last Abbot of Bangor, that we are indebted for the establishment of a church at Worthenbury; he assisted his father in the work of the monastery at Bangor, and he founded the abbey in Carnarvonshire, which is called Bangor Deiniol, after him. It was made a bishopric by Mael gwon Gwynedd, a Prince of Britain, who endowed the see of Bangor with lands and franchises. Deiniol became the first bishop, and was buried at Bardsey, which in some way was connected with Bangor Iscoyd; indeed, I think it was an offshoot from it.

Mr. Williams says there is great difficulty in assigning an exact date to this, but as Bangor Monastery was in its most flourishing condition about the end of the 7th century, I think we shall not be far wrong in saying that Worthenbury Church was founded fully 1,200 years ago. Our present church is the successor in the third or fourth degree of the original church wherein our forefathers worshipped God, and listened to the teaching of the monks of Bangor; and after the lapse of twelve centuries our church, dedicated to St. Deiniol, is a constant reminder to the parish of that good man.

Of the special history of Worthenbury at this period there is no record; it is to be presumed that it progressed in civilisation like other parts of

England and Wales. The Welsh or British name for it was Gurthymp, meaning Emerald. By a common transition the letter G has been changed into W, hence Worthenbury. It is very possible that this district got its name from the rich colour of its pastures, and anyone looking on the meadows on approaching Worthenbury either from England or Wales, must acknowledge that the name is still appropriate.

From the date of Domesday Book, which was ordered to be made by William the Conqueror, and completed in 1086, we have an authentic history of Worthenbury as far as it goes. The original volumes are still in existence, and I saw them in the Record Office, Chancery Lane, less than two years ago. Flintshire was brought under the rule of the Conqueror, and Maelor Saesneg is included in the Hundred called Dudestan, as the whole county was then added to the Palatinate of Chester.

Domesday Book is written in Latin, and is most difficult to read. I have before me now the original words, concerning Hurdingberie, as it is called, but I will only give an English translation of it:—" This

same Robert holds Hurdingberic. Earl Edwin held
it. There are v. hides rateable to the Gelt. The
land is x. carucates, and there are one serf and 3
Villeins, and 3 foreigners, and a radman with 3
carucates. There is a new mill here, and an acre of
meadow. Of this Manor a Knight holds a hide and
a half, and he, with his men, has one carucate there.
In King Edward's time it was worth 13 ores, which
the Villeins paid; it is now worth 30 shillings. The
Earl found it waste. He has a (wood) 2 leagues in
length, and one in width." By way of explanation
of the above I may say that a carucate of land was
as much as an ordinary yoke of oxen would plough
in a year.

The Earl Edwin mentioned was the last Mercian
Earl of Chester. He took part against William the
Conqueror, who defeated him and gave the county
Palatine of Chester to his nephew, Hugh Lupus, " to
hold freely by the sword as he held England by the
crown." Hugh Lupus divided his earldom into four
baronies, and appointed Robert Fitz-Hugh to rule
over one of them, named the Barony of Malpas. It
is very probable that the old Cheshire Hundred of
Dodleston or Dudestan is the one to which the

Hundred of Maelor Saesneg was annexed, and as the Barony of Malpas was in this Hundred, now called Broxton, the Robert who held Hurdingberie is easily identified as the above named Robert Fitz-Hugh. The King Edward mentioned is Edward the Confessor.

The land of this parish was subject to the tax called the Dane Gelt, first paid in 991 to bribe the Danes not to ravage England. A hide of land was supposed to be 120 acres of land fit to plough.

When William the Conqueror was established on the throne of England he rewarded his Norman knights, as well as his Saxon adherents, with grants of land in every part of his dominions, replacing with loyal friends and supporters the old lords of the soil, who had been in arms against him. These knights became naturalised Englishmen, and in many cases married the daughters of the former owners of their lands, and became as much English in heart and feeling as if their forefathers had been born in the land. They were, however, a warlike race, and ever ready to engage in any border warfare that was going on — the old Britons in the Principality of Wales generally found them a congenial employ-

5

ment of this kind. Noble and gallant as the struggle was on the part of Wales to preserve its independence, yet it was ineffectual, and it was compelled to surrender to the superior force of Edward I. in 1282.

With one of Edward's Norman families the story of Worthenbury is so much mixed up that it is impossible to avoid a frequent mention of it; moreover, the greater part of the materials for the historical gleanings which I am putting together, is taken from the records of this family. These papers date back 600 years, are in wonderful preservation, and refer not only to subjects of family but public interest. The first mention I can find of Emral is that the lord of Dînas Brân left a widow whose dower house was Emral, which was said to be built for her. Some people derive the name from this—Emma's Hall.

Soon, however, as I have already shown, the Pulestons came to Emral, another name for which is Embers Hall, from its having been so constantly burned by the Welsh, but since there are no records of these burnings, or any allusion to them in the old papers, this derivation must be put aside. The name in olden days has been written in various ways, as Embrall, Emerall, Emerault.

It seems of interest to record that Robert Puleston, who was born about 1358, married Lewri, daughter of Griffith Fechan, sister of Owen Glendower. He forfeited the Emral estate for joining in his brother-in-law's rebellion, and was slain 1 Henry IV. Owen Glendower was closely connected with this country by being prince of the country beyond Llangollen, called, I believe, Glendowerdy. In him rested the representation of three sovereign lines of princes, of Powys, North and South Wales. He married a daughter of Sir David Hanmer, which would make him a friend of Robert Puleston's. Probably many a good yeoman and archer of Worthenbury fell when he was slain. His estates were afterwards restored. Owen Glendower also owned the Fenns Wood as Prince of Powys, which had, however, been cleared of its timber in or about 1193.

Our next bit of authentic information about Emral is taken from a will found among the old papers there. It is written on parchment, and is in excellent preservation. On the back of the will is the official probate and letter of administration, dated in the Parish Church of Bangor, 17th April, 1444. The following is a translation of it :—

In the name of God, Amen. On the 20th day of February in the year of our Lord 1443, I, John de Pulleston, of sound mind and healthy memory and being sick in body, make my will in this manner, first I bequeath my soul to the omnipotent God and to the blessed Virgin His Mother and to all His Saints and my body to be buried in the chapel of St. Thomas the Martyr, at Emrall. Also I bequeath for the repair of the Parish Church of Bangor, 5 shillings, also I bequeath for the repair of the Chapel of Owton (Overton) Madoc, 5 shillings, also I bequeath for the repair of the Chapel of Worthenbre, 6s. 8d., also I bequeath to Margaret, my daughter, £20, also I bequeath to my daughter, Katherine, £20 to marry them. Also I bequeath to Sir Howell, Chaplain of Bangor, 2s. 6d., also I bequeath to John Syden, Chaplain of Worthenbre, 3s. 4d., also I bequeath and give all the residue of my goods not before bequeathed to Angharat, the daughter of Griffith, my wife, and to Roger, my son, also I declare and make and appoint as my executrixes, Angharat, daughter of Griffith, my wife, Margaret and Katherine, my daughters, that they having God before their eyes may perform and fulfil in all respects this my present will. And I also declare and appoint John Troubrake, Chamberlain of Chester, Griffith Hannen (Hanmer), Robert Trevor, and Madoc ap Robert, overseers of my said will that they may diligently see that my present will is executed in due manner.

These being witnesses Richard ap Madoc and others given at Emrall the day and year above mentioned.

This will proves that the Chapel at Emral was consecrated, while at the same time it tells there was a chapel and Chaplain at Worthenbury, and he gives the same rank of Chaplain to the officiating clergymen of Bangor and Worthenbury. It seems reasonable to infer from the bequests he made that though Bangor was at all events the Mother Church of Emral Chapel if not of Worthenbury, yet he looked on both of these as having greater claims on the Pulestons than Bangor.

About 1479, Lewis Glyn Cothi, a celebrated bard who wrote at this time, addressed one of his poems to Roger, son of John, most probably the John and Roger mentioned in the above mentioned will, and speaks of Emral by name and calls it a noble mansion, and calls Roger the hero of the poem and head of the family, " a great warrior and a worthy descendant of his great ancestor, Sir Roger Puleston, Kt."

At this time England was suffering from the horrors of civil war ; for thirty years the country was split up into conflicting factions, and the rival houses of York and Lancaster had their adherents in almost every home of any importance in the kingdom, many of the nobility and gentry taking part in the struggle. John Puleston espoused the Lancastrian cause and was a devoted follower of Margaret of Anjou ; he, together with John and William Hanmer and others were impeached for aiding the Duke of Somerset to escape after the Battle of Barnet, in 1471.

The fact of the Pulestons being engaged on the Lancastrian side, perhaps accounts for the circumstance of a manuscript book being found at Emral containing sixty-six contemporary copies of Queen Margaret's letters and proclamations. It is also said

that a Puleston was one of Queen Margaret's maids
of honour. The discovery of these MSS. and deeds
was only made in 1861, when a vast mass of documents dating from Edward I. to the beginning of the
present century, the accumulation of hundreds of
years, were found in a heap under the finely timbered
roof of the Old Mansion House, and though known
by some to be there, they were looked upon as useless
lumber; no letter or copy of a letter of Queen
Margaret's was known to exist, as her friends were
tortured to give up all documents relating to her;
the Camden Society when they heard of this
"treasure trove," asked and obtained leave to print
them.

In 1471, 49 Henry VI.—9 Edward IV., Jasper
Earl of Pembroke, appoints Roger a Pylston Viscount
of Flint on 6th December—a remarkable date, as
Henry only regained power from December, 1470, to
May, 1471. There are two letters from this Earl of
Pembroke to Roger Puleston, Governor of Denbigh
Castle, one of which is addressed "To the right
trusty and well beloved Roger a Puleston and to
John Eyton, or either of them.—Right trusty and
well beloved cousins and friends, we greet you well,

and suppose you have in yr. remembrance the great dishonour and rebuke that we and ye now of late have had by Traitors March (Edward Earl of March, King Edward IV.) and Herbert (William Herbert Earl of Pembroke), with other affinities, as well as in letting us of our journey to the King, as in putting my father (Owen Tudor, husband to Queen Catherine), your kinsman, to death and their traitorous demeaning. We propose, therefore, with the might of our Lord, and the assistance of you and others, our kinsmen and friends, within short time to avenge. Trusting verily that ye be well willed and put your hands unto the same, and of your disposition with your good advice therein, we pray you to ascertain, etc., in all haste possible, as our especial trust is in you. Written at the town of Tenby, 26th February, J. PEMBROCK."

Probably this and a second letter desiring him to keep Denbigh Castle for the King, and to get in all the revenue he could, were written in 1470. This letter, from the date of it and the quaintness of its style, I have ventured to put in here, though the matter of it is not connected with Worthenbury. I have, however, spared the reader the old spelling. One of

the Pulestons was in the household of Henry VIII.
It is supposed that "the Book of the Court," now
in my possession, came through him.   Pages might
be written of the Pulestons, their marriages, children,
and law suits, but nothing is recorded at this period
directly connected with the Parish of Worthenbury,
but I will tell what Leland wrote three centuries
ago of this district :—

"English Maelor lieth altogether on the south
side of the river Dee, containing 3 'paroches,'
Oureton, Bangor Vaur, Hanmer.   The 'paroches'
be very great, and they have some chapels.   There
was a great pile or castel at Oureton in ancient
time, which was thrown down by the violence of the
Dee changing its bottom, for of old time Dee ran
half a mile from the castle in a slave of the valley
called Whistan, where now is wood and ploughed
ground right again Oureton.   The town of Oureton
hath had Burgesses, but now there is not twenty
houses.   One part of the ditches and hill of the
castle yet remaineth ; the residence is in the bottom
of Dee."   Then follows a description of Bangor,
which has already been quoted : "Beneath Bangor,
still lower on the south side of river Dee, is a parish

called ' Worthembre,' in Welsh, Guothumbre, having a ' faire church but as a member to Bangor.'

" Hanmer Parish lieth south-east of Oureton, Bangor and Worthembre, but so that these three lie betwixt it and river Dee, and some part of this joineth Whitchurch Parish in Shropshire, but in the ' edge of Cheshire and upon Malpasse.' This Hanmer is a very large parish, and hath a deal more riches in it than the residue of English Maelor. In Oureton is ' meatly good woode, corn and pasture, and standeth on somewhat higher ground than Bangor and Worthembre.' Bangor hath good corn and pasture, but little or no wood, and lieth all in valleys ; and in Worthembre no wood, but good corn and pasture. By Hanmer Church is a great pool, about a mile in length and half a mile in breadth, and every gentleman there hath his fair pool. There is ' forty gentilman in this paroche that have praty lands : Pilston Knight hath much land in Hanmere, but his chief house is in Worthem- bre paroche at a place called Emerhaule.' Hanmer Knight dwelleth at Hanmere, and in that paroche be aliquot Hanmers that hath lands. There is a great moor in Hanmer called of some the Fenns.

Dymock dwelleth at Haulghton. Edward Pilston, son to the Knight, dwelleth in Oureton paroche at Coitegolle. Ellys ap Richard dwelleth in Bangor at Alre on Dee, south side, a 'fayre' house. John Broughton dwelleth in Worthembre paroche at Broughton. All this English Maelor, though it lie not hard on Flintshire, but hath Welsh Maelor betwixt it and Flint, yet it 'longeth to Flintshire, and they come to the sessions to Flint, yet have they liberty, in token of the old castle, to keep a prisoner in Oureton three days, and so to send him to Flint.'"

Many and great changes have taken place in Worthembre in the three centuries since this was written, and now we have an ordnance survey which exactly shows us the present condition of the parish. In it there are 3,419 acres, of which 3,322 are land, fifty-one roads, and forty-five water. The extreme length is from Adravelyn to the most distant meadow adjoining the Parish of Shocklach, called on the tithe map Cae Leasa, is about four miles and a quarter, and the greatest width rather more than two miles. It is bounded by the Parishes of Bangor, Penley, Hanmer, and Threapwood, which is partly

in Flintshire and partly in Cheshire: The river Dee
separates it from Denbighshire, and a small brook,
called Llandegs Brook, from England, and the
Province of York from the Province of Canterbury.
There are two meadows in the midst of Worthenbury land in the Parish of Bangor and in the county
of Denbigh, though on the English side of the river
Dee, they are called the Island and the Little
Island, and by the end of the Island is the former
bed of the river Dee, which is locally known as Old
Dee.

Curiously there are two meadows on the Welsh
side of the river Dee which belong to Worthenbury
and Flintshire, called the Roydens Hall Meadows.
A change in the river Dee caused this oddity, but
when it happened there is no tradition; possibly it
took place when the " Castel " at Oureton was
destroyed, and the river Dee seized the site on
which it was built. There is, however, no record
of this event, and the only thing that keeps alive
the remembrance of it there, is a wood at Brynypys
called the Castle Wood. As Maelor is called the
Border Hundred, so Worthenbury may be called the
Border Parish. On crossing Llandegs Brook one

may easily have one foot in England and the other in Wales, so narrow is the boundary there between the two countries. Then one foot would be in the Diocese of Chester, while the other would be in that of St. Asaph. The boundary between the Parishes of Bangor and Worthenbury is equally narrow in two places a mile from each other.

Leland's statement that in Worthembre " was no wood " must not be taken literally, as there are still at Broughton some few remaining trees of Thrape Wood, and probably there would be many more 300 years ago. Those now mentioned must have been then in their prime, as it is very evident that they have weathered many a storm since his day. Burton's Wood, too, which covers an area of about forty acres, was of such importance 200 years ago as to be specially mentioned in a survey of the Emral property, and must have been well grown in those days, as it afterwards required the expense and trouble of an Act of Parliament to cut down the fine timber which grew in it. The present trees there are said to have sprung from the old stools. Leland probably only meant that Worthenbury, then as now, was more celebrated for its meadows and pastures than its woodlands. No doubt, as corn and grazing land increased in value, forest after forest disappeared in England as they do now in New Zealand before the axe of the clearer of the soil. Then the wolf and wild boar were destroyed, and the deer alone left for the kings and nobles to hunt. The fox and the badger were tormented by terriers in their earths, for fox hunting as it is now conducted did not commence till the end of the reign of George II. There is, however, an entry in the parish register of Worthenbury in 1598, " John Robert the huntesman of Emrall was buried the nine and twentieth of Januarie." This tells us the country squires even then had hunting of some sort, and John Robert was huntsman at Emrall to Sir Roger Puleston, who married a daughter of Sir George Bromley. This Sir Roger was M.P. for Denbigh, 1592, and Sheriff of Flint, 1598; he was knighted by James I. 1617, at Gerards Bromley, and died the following year. His portrait is in the possession of the present baronet.

Worthenbury is a grass parish, and the chief produce of the agriculturist is cheese, this has now been the case for many years, though during the Peninsular War, when wheat was often £1 a bushel, a good deal of the old pastures and some of the Dee meadows were broken up with the plough, but since free trade has pulled the price of wheat down to a £1 per quarter, the land is again bright and green. There is one very curious custom in Worthenbury which has prevailed time out of mind, which is, that a considerable portion of the meadow land belonging to the Emral Estate is retained in hand, the owner paying rates and taxes and other expenses and then selling by auction the hay and after grass. There are numberless bills among the Emral papers of 1730 connected with this custom, and a curious letter from one, Charles Price, dated, Shocklach, 23rd December, 1772, to Mrs. Parry Price, the mother and guardian of Richard, afterwards created a Baronet by George III. who was then a minor, saying : " In regard to the meadow rents they commonly have been proclaimed in the churchyards of Worthenbury, Shocklach, and I believe Malpas, ten days or so before, and I think Sunday next would be a most proper time for notice."

There were then no daily papers, and this gives us an insight into the primitive habits of those days, though the last century had only thirty years to run. The hay has been carried off these meadows for centuries without depreciating their value ; the river Dee fertilising them by its floods, which, however, are not an unmixed good, as they sometimes come when they are not wanted and in some years carry away to Chester the produce of the year which was intended for the winter keep of the tenants' cows.

There are three brooks running in part through Worthenbury, though they become one before they reach the village, one of these is known in the parish as the Wyche Brook, though the map dignifies it with the name of the river Elf, it takes its rise at Quoisley, where there is a pool, and passing through the Wyches is utilised in driving the wheels of three corn mills, one of which has just been burned down (March, 1895). Almost in the memory of man there were salt works in these Wyches. There is also a small stream called the Pandy Brook which, however, soon loses itself in a larger one in Emral Park ; this rises at Black Mere, in Shropshire, and runs through Emral Park, close to the Hall, and after joining the Elf about 100 yards from the county bridge over the

Malpas and Wrexham road, runs through the meadows until it reaches the Dee.

The rise of the waters of the Dee is always watched with some anxiety in spring and autumn, when commonly there are a great many cattle grazing the meadows; and it is wonderful how rapidly the water sometimes fills the deep banks of the river, especially when the waters of Bala Pool are forced by a strong wind into the Dee. Sometimes, too, a flood comes from the wicked little Elf without the Dee being very high. Formerly, the cottagers living in the meadows were obliged to live in their upper rooms when the meadows were flooded, and come in coracles to the village for supplies of food; but these cottages have been re-built by their present owner, and now the dwellers in them are not driven from their kitchens. At the very end of the year 1862 we had a terrible experience of what Dee in flood can do. Day after day the rain descended in torrents, which caused the banks of the Whitchurch and Ellesmere Canal to break, this poured down the valley into our brooks and caused a disastrous flood; a bridge at Emral was destroyed, and the two waterfalls in the park greatly damaged and one swept away

6

Again, in 1872, on the 18th June, there was a remarkable flood caused by a terrific thunder storm and deluges of rain, which literally flooded the roads. Between two and three o'clock a.m. the stone bridge of three arches at the entrance of the village over the river Elf gave way by the force of the water; one half fell, having split, the other half was useless for anything but foot people. The result was a new bridge of one arch, not so picturesque as the old one, but as the span is of larger dimensions, far better calculated to take the heavy waters of the Elf to the Dee.

When the present bridge was supposed to be completed, the architect ordered the scaffold centre to be removed; as the mortar was not quite dry, we who stood by heard a grating sound, which. however, happily soon ceased, but the sinking of the arch is and always will be very apparent on the upper side, as long as the bridge lasts. The history of the old bridge, or rather bridges, is recorded on the stones taken from these bridges, and now built into the present one. On the oldest stone was carved " This bridge, being a county bridge, formerly built of timber, was rebuilt of stone at the county charge by Samuel Davies and John Baker, of the city of Chester, masons, in the year 1729, Thomas Puleston, of Emrall, and Broughton Whitehall, of Broughton, Esquires, being trustees for, and Thomas Hughes and John Poyser, gentlemen, supervisors of the said work."

Another stone tells that " This bridge was widened at the east end by the same architect under the direction of Richard Puleston, Esq., of Emrall, and the Rev. W. Whitehall Davies, of Broughton." On the new bridge there is this inscription : " This bridge was erected at the expense of the county of Flint in the year of our Lord 1872-73 to replace one destroyed by a flood on the 18th June, 1872, from plans drawn by H. J. Fairclough, architect, St. Asaph, W. Williams, contractor, Rhyl, under the personal superintendence of R. Howard, Esq., of Broughton, and the Rev. T. H. G. Puleston, of Worthenbury."

The cost of this bridge and raising the road considerably on the Wrexham side was about £1,800.

Since I have been living in the parish, though before I became Rector, three other bridges have been built, one over the Queen's Ford, another over

Turpin's Ford, and a third going into the meadows, the only way into them formerly being down the brook for about 100 yards. The story I heard as to the building of the bridge over Turpin's Ford is somewhat singular. A tenant complained that he was afraid he should be drowned there, adding that he was apt to take occasionally a drop too much to drink, and that then the ford was dangerous; it was pointed out to him that he could remedy this by drinking less, but this seemed so unlikely to succeed that he shook his head; so this, as well as the other two bridges were built, the second Sir Richard Puleston contributing liberally towards the expense.

Worthenbury consists of only one township, which is composed of four hamlets, Wallington, Broughton, Mulsford, and Wern. Owing to so much of the land being laid down to pasture, the population has gradually decreased. As far as my memory carries me, it was 631 in 1851, while by the census of 1891 there were 419 residents, of whom 285 were of the gentler sex, living in ninety-four houses. Several houses have been taken down and never rebuilt, including the mill at Emral and the house adjoining, in the middle of the last century. There was

also in the memory of men I have known, a farm-
house close to the Malpas entrance to Broughton
Hall, an old oak tree up to the road marking the
boundary of the farm-yard. There have also been
three cottages in the parish burned down which have
not been rebuilt, two of them in a meadow called
the Bradshaws, on the Malpas Road, and one just on
the outskirts of the parish close to the Cottage Gorse.

The village itself is much as it was in size 200
years ago. The houses in it, with four exceptions, are
modern—undoubtedly the most picturesque building
in it, is an old black and white dwelling, with pretty
gables and thatched roof, occupied and owned by
my kind and good neighbour, Miss Beavan. Perhaps the house occupied by Mr. and Miss Dawson
is a building of more pretensions ; the parlour ceiling,
too, is curiously ornamented with a design in relief,
somewhat after the style of some of the grand old
ceilings at Emral. It was here that the Pulestons
of Worthenbury lived, a junior branch of the Emral
family. There are frequent entries in the parish
register about 200 years ago of baptisms and burials
of members of this family, which, however, is now
extinct.

There is, nearer the meadows, another brick and timber cottage which has been restored, the old timber being left in it just as it was before the Commonwealth. A few years ago the Emral Arms was a quaint specimen of the old roadside inn, with a sign which bore the family arms, with a bit of fox hunting thrown in, probably to suit the taste of the well known " Ned " Bate, who for a great many years occupied the position of " mine host " there, after having served for more than thirty years the first Sir Richard Puleston as huntsman to his foxhounds. This veteran sportsman died 4th March, 1853, in his eighty-third year. The following lines were written to his memory by a friend of the writer of this, who delighted to hear some of the old man's reminiscences of the last century :—

" Amid the ancient fields let the aged huntsman rest
　With old familiar faces and the voices he loved best,
　And as ye pass his quiet bed ye need not mourn or weep,
　For after his long day of life, old Ned perforce must sleep.

" And if he dreams what cause of wail, the sounds are sweet
　　　he hears,
　Sad wintry winds with Dee in flood make music in his ears,
　For mingling with their fitful roar is borne the deep wild cry
　That tells the painted hounds have found, and the red fox he
　　　must die.

" But if the Hunt should come that way, let strength pause in
   his pride,
And youthful vigour in its flush, for one moment turn aside
And gaze on the old man's grave, ye will not ride less well
If ye can kindly say, Old Ned, calm be thy bed, farewell."

Besides Ned Bate there are many well known and
respected inhabitants of Worthenbury who deserve
a place in a history of the parish. The one who
merits the pride of place is now alive, and the only
person who is alive whom I shall venture to write of
in this book ; I mean Charles Richards. The reason
I make him an exception is, because he belongs to
an older generation, though I am pleased to say he is
still among us, and well and hearty, and sent me a
message a short time ago, after I had called and found
him out, that he was very well and had not an
ache or a pain ; and so to all appearance he is
well, as my wife saw him about a year ago, up
a ladder gathering his apples ! and even now
(March, 1895) he lives quite alone, merely having
a kind neighbour to come in and " do " for him,
and yet he was born in 1798, while George III.
had still twenty-two years to reign, and whose Jubilee
he remembers quite as well as he does that of good
Queen Victoria.

In early life he was, in some capacity, in the service of Mr. Whitehall Davies, of Broughton, who generously left him a pension, which he has enjoyed for about sixty years. All his life has been spent in Worthenbury, and for a great many years he occupied a farm on the Broughton Estate, succeeding, I think, Mr. Pritchard, than whom no one was more respected by his neighbours, though Mr. Poyser, who also lived under the same kind landlord, would run him very close. Charles Richards lost his wife some years ago, but not until they had celebrated their golden wedding. Perhaps the best known inhabitant of Worthenbury in my early days was Henry Crane, who, with his wife Mary, lived at Brook Cottage: he was born in the parish and was a son of "Old" Crane, who was steward at Emral, in which office Henry Crane succeeded him. He was always ready to undertake any work for the good of the parish, and was much respected. He and his wife lie in our churchyard. His brother Edward lived at Emral Lodge Farm until he died; a kinder man or better neighbour never lived, or one more considerate to the poor; both these brothers as far as I am able to judge consistently did their duty. Henry was the better known of the two, as he was constantly seen in the hunting field, where he generally was right in the front. Neither of them left children, so that now the name of Crane, once, and for about a century, as familiar as a household word in the parish, is nearly forgotten.

The Dawsons I have incidentally mentioned—father and son, they have lived for about a century in the parish ; which seemed to agree very well with John Dawson, the father of the present Dawsons, as he told this deponent shortly before his death, when he was about eighty, that he had " never taken a dose of physic in his life, except once, and then he was bitten by a mad dog." He was rather a short man, but a very plucky one : for sitting up one night with a cow " faring " to calve, he saw a light in the church just opposite his window, and on going in found that a man of the name of Parker had broken into the church and the Puleston vault, and was stealing the fittings of the coffins. He fetched his son " Tommy," who was about 6 ft. 5 in., and one of them went for the parish constable, my old friend James Clutton, and, I think, George Griffiths — the Worthenbury blacksmith before I came to the parish—and between them they secured Parker, who was of much the same height as "Tommy Dawson," and I saw him sentenced to penal servitude for some years, from which he did not live to return.

The Dawsons had near relatives also in the parish, whose family had lived 100 years on the Emral Estate, James and Job Parry; both died at Mulsford Hall Farm. No two men were more respected than these brothers; finer men, too, are seldom seen. James was an old bachelor, and a sister kept house for him; he loved hard work, and though very well off, almost to the end of his days, he would plough or mow, as if he could not afford to employ anyone to work for him. Poor fellow, at the last he was paralysed, and had several apoplectic seizures, which perhaps did not surprise his medical man, as he always had toasted cheese for supper, except when they had pork pies in the house! He died universally regretted, and then his brother Job, whom he greatly loved, succeeded him at Mulsford Hall, where he also died; he was probably James' heir, as he never married. The Moyles, of the Gates Farm, were before my time, and I can only just remember the

Sadliers living there; to them the Fearnalls succeeded, who were so well known and respected in their day, as I am thankful to add are all their children.

Mr. Fearnall died at the Gates Farm, when his wife migrated to one close to Worthenbury Rectory: she was one of those gracious, heavenly minded women, whom it is a privilege to know. I went to see her on her death bed, and her bright face carried an assurance of future happiness.

James Clutton and his wife lived for many years where my good neighbour Richard Huxley now lives in the village. Clutton suffered heavily by the rinderpest, which was a fearful scourge in this parish, as it killed nearly 600 head of cattle, and taking a gloomy view of a probability of a return of the pestilence, left the parish, as also did Robert Davies, of Wallington Farm, from the same cause.

For many years, Thomas Jones, of Wallington, was one of the most useful men in the parish, as he was ever ready to serve the office of churchwarden or do anything he could for any one. Poor fellow, he was killed by falling from a load of hay and broke his back.

The family of Morris lived at Brook Farm when I

first knew the parish ; they held the farm for three lives, and then when the last life fell in they left ; they were, however, almost unknown to me.

Philip Gregory, who lived at Dol Ennion Farm, I scarcely knew ; he was a very good sort, and was succeeded by his brother. The Matthews, of Adravelyn, and the Devonports, were almost unknown to me, except by name. But well do I remember Thomas Matthews, of the Holly Bush Farm ; a very kind hearted, good man he was, full of that charity which thinketh no evil. It seems extraordinary how little is known of any family of a country parish, or even the house they lived in, after they have left the parish or the house is pulled down. It is on this account that I have put in the names of the most prominent of the occupiers of farms in the parish that have come within my knowledge.

It always seemed to me that there were in Worthenbury an extraordinary number of old people. So much was this the case indeed in my early days that William Croome, who was married in the parish, was wont to say, " The people of Worthenbury lived as long as they liked ; " and then

they seemed to retain their bodily powers far beyond
the three score years and ten allotted to man.   One
of these, Gregory, an octogenarian, lived at the
Sarn.   I was pointing him out as a good specimen
of an old man, when he demurred, saying, " I am not
half the man I was, I am getting old fast," to which
I replied, " Well, I don't know that, you walked to
Chester and back about a fortnight ago, I believe,"
which he admitted he did : not much change out of
thirty-two miles !

Thomas Large, who lived on a small farm at
Wallington, was another good fair octogenarian.
When he complained on a certain occasion to me of
not feeling at all well, I asked him how old he was,
implying that that possibly might be the cause ; he
at once scouted the idea and said emphatically,
" tinna that."   For many years we had among us
Edward Humphreys, who was one of my show old
men.   He had been a soldier, and had seen some
service in the Peninsular War, and had a medal with
the inscription, " British Army, 1793-1804."   He
gave a graphic account of one of the engagements
he had been in, with the words of his commanding
officer, with a few expletives thrown in.   His account

of this battle might possibly differ from that given in Napier's " Peninsular War ;" but without doubt he would have said his was the correct one.

What a revolution time has worked in the dress of our labourers ! Who that saw the well dressed, neat black clothes of our labourers to-day, at church or a funeral, could possibly imagine that they were the immediate successors of those who did the manual labour of this parish forty years ago ? My mind's eye now sees Dick Jervis, an old man well on in the seventies, appearing at church Sunday after Sunday in an old blue tailed coat with an exceedingly high collar and gilt buttons, and to protect this valuable relic, he wore a white smock frock, which was pulled off and left in the belfry during the service. When his hat, which was of a shape " not worn now," was taken off, he showed a head as bare as a billiard ball, which he then covered with an old yellow wig. When coming to church Dick always walked first, while his wife Ann followed at a respectful distance. Tommy Beavan, another of about the same age, and Jenny his wife, who generally spoke her mind very plainly, were in their way quite as quaint, and the same may be said of Dicky Boote and old John Roberts, who was in my early days dog feeder at Emral.

The oldest man I can recollect was William Almond. He and his sister, Betty Ellis, lived in a little mud hut in Wallington Lane, which has tumbled down ages ago. William was born, I believe, in George's II. reign, and said that he recollected the mill at Emral being pulled down, as well as the Chapel. One of the greatest characters that I have known in the parish was Nanney Bridge. She was a pattern of neatness and cleanliness. In those days she was about the only cottager who kept cows ; she made excellent toasting cheeses, which usually all went to Emral, or "the family," as she called us. Her husband, William Bridge, had been coachman at Emral. I have heard he was a very neat, sober, decent man, but I never saw him. She had an only son, Henry, who long survived her—a quiet, inoffensive man, but one who had not much "drive," as they say in Cheshire, about him.

Nanney Bridge was succeeded in part of the cottage she held by Mary Pitt, who was a very striving, industrious woman. Her husband was in a consumption for about five years, and no one could have supposed he would have lived five months ; poor fellow, he was very grateful for the attention he received from me, and, to my great astonishment, had two panes of glass put in my hall door with my two family crests on them, which remain there to the present moment. Very few, I think, in the parish will now remember Ellis Jones, who lived at the Wern, and looked after the meadows belonging to the Emral estate for about fifty years. He was an honest, industrious old man, but was blessed with a temper. When this was "out," he would not speak to anyone. A story is told that on one occasion he had not spoken to his wife for two days, and the poor woman could stand this no longer, so she bustled about the house as if she was searching diligently for something, and then swept a jug off the table, on which Ellis broke out, " Woman, what are you looking for ? " " Your tongue," was her reply.

Two old people at the Sarn, too, amused me some-times with their squabbles, for which on one occasion I was remonstrating with them, when the wife broke out, " Well, Sir, he is such a mon you can neither scrat him nor claw him," and the daughter, who was an elderly woman, seemed to second this, and added. " He's a most undutiful father." When I first became Rector, John Edwards was clerk and sexton, and had been in office for ages, succeeding, I think, one Elias Roberts, who had acted for time out of mind as parish clerk. Elias was dead, but his widow, a very old woman about ninety, was alive, and lived with her son, who was a shoemaker. It was from him that I got hold of the old informal book of parish entries, which is now in our iron chest.

John Edwards, who came of a highly respected family, was certainly of a type which is unknown now—very good and reverent he was, though he would occasionally have forty winks in the afternoon service and during morning prayers, as once when the Rev. Lloyd Fletcher was reading prayers the old clerk was lost, on which my reverend friend, who was also somewhat of a character, said in a stage whisper, " Mr. Clerk, you are in the evening service." I have a daguerreotype of the old man. which is accurate, though not flattering.

James and Betty Prince and James and Betty Meredith were all in their way worthy of mention.

7

some of these did not know a "black letter," but they had a simple faith and reverence for holy things, which the present generation is perhaps deficient in. When I first lived with my father at Emral, Daniel Cooper was head gardener. He was a shrewd, canny Scot, very clever in his business and very honest. Many a time were we in those days out together after the trouts, and generally he was too many for them ; when with spectacles on the end of his nose, and perhaps the keenest black eyes behind them you ever saw, he dropped his short line into the brook. When he died, Thomas Poynton, who had worked for some thirty years in the gardens at Emral, succeeded him, until he, too, passed away, and Edmund Cooper, the son, and the widow soon followed the good old man. Joseph Walker, a rare stamp, did the Rectory garden as long as he was able to work, and carried one back to long past days by his quaint expressions. As an example, he always spoke of the approach to the Rectory as the Coach Road. Joseph and Ann Bebbington succeeded him, both hard working people of a type that is lost. Sammy Stokes and his sister lived for many years in Wallington Lane. He was stone deaf, but his old sister, Miss Stokes, was as sharp as they make them. On one occasion I went to see her; she made me laugh by telling me that a clerk from a solicitor's office had been to pay her some money, for which she signed the receipt and bade the gentleman good-bye, on which he said, "If you will bring the money to our office we will invest it for you." "Oh," she replied, "you want to riddle it, do you?" Nearer the present day were John and Elizabeth Webb, both hard working, kind people, who were ever ready to do a good turn to any neighbour, and were deeply interested in everything in the parish, and especially in the church. They died within twelve hours of each other, having been man and wife for about forty years, and their death cast quite a gloom for a time through the parish; they left an example of unpretending duty which all of us may follow with advantage. They had two especial friends in "our village," who had originally come with them from Shawbury, in Shropshire, a brother and sister, James and Maria Howell. These worthy people had been for years in service, and by care and industry had saved a good deal of money for people in their station. My old friend Maria left £50 to the poor of Worthenbury, as well as various sums to other charitable purposes. James followed his sister's lead as to Shawbury and Salop Infirmary, and also left the rector of Worthenbury £20 free of legacy duty, thinking, I hope, that he would apply it to a good purpose.

Since I have been rector of this parish three parishioners have literally died in my arms, the first being the wife of William Matthews, who lived in the village opposite "The Prince and Princess of Wales' Oak." Her husband was a son of Robert Matthews, coachman to Mr. Whitehall Davies, of Broughton, and one of his pensioners; he, however, has passed away long ago. Another of these was Thomas Moore, a fine specimen of an Englishman. He was gamekeeper at Emral for about forty years to my father and myself. His sayings were very quaint, and he had, I believe, not one enemy in the parish. The third was Tom Wynne, who was a blacksmith at the Sarn. He had a rather hard shell, but the kernel was one of the tenderest I ever met with. I do not think he could have done an unkind thing by anyone. It was for him I built the cottage where old Thomas Beavan's stood, in which his daughter Deborah and her husband, Harry Richards, now live. Levi Huxley, a kindly, good neighbour, was present when Wynne died.

Education, when I came to Worthenbury, was at a very low ebb, both in Worthenbury and elsewhere in this neighbourhood. Lord Kenyon, the second peer, was the first gentleman in modern times who seemed to take any interest in it. He built a school at Penley, another at Threapwood, and, I think, one at Hanmer. In more modern times still, perhaps Worthenbury first took up the work. When I came here there was a very little narrow room and a small school kept by a good old man by the name of Jones, but he was then a confirmed invalid and a perfect martyr to rheumatic gout, so much so that really his daughter, Elizabeth Bate, was school mistress. She was excellent as a needle woman, and she, I believe, carried on the school for a short time after her father's death.

In 1849, however, we got from a training college a Miss Milstead, but I believe she was promoted in 1850. She was succeeded by Miss Chapman. The money, however, was small that we could then raise,

as we only paid these school mistresses £36 per
annum and £6 per annum for their lodgings, and of
course their travelling expenses. However, we soon
found that we wanted a master, and when our present
school-room was built we got one, and have from
that time to the present taken a creditable position
among the schools of the diocese.

In 1888 a new class-room was added at an expense
of £100, £40 of which was paid by Mr. Howard, of
Broughton, £40 by myself, and £20 by Lord Kenyon,
as his property in the parish was less than ours.

I must add one thought of my own when writing
of the School and Parish of Worthenbury, which I
do in the hope that it may make our cottagers to-day
more contented with the times in which they live.
We often hear of the good old times. If any one
remembers, as I do, the wretchedness of the homes
of our labourers, their constant struggle for the bare
necessaries of life, for luxuries they had none, they
would learn to bless and thank God for their im-
proved condition ; and now is added a free education
for their children and a large share in the local and
Parliamentary government of their country.

I have already quoted Leland as saying, "John

Broughton dwelleth in Worthembre Paroche at Broughton." This is one of the chief houses in the parish, and is said to have been built in the reign of Henry VII., when we first read of the Broughtons of Broughton. The house is a very fine example of the old Cheshire style of brick and timber, with this peculiarity that it has never been painted black and white as is commonly the fashion with houses of this character. The south and west fronts are very much the same as when Leland wrote the above. The additions and alterations on the northern side were made by Mr. Whitehall Davies early in the present century, and in no way interfere with the old building. The porch was, however, built by the present owner, and since it exactly preserves the character of the old house, if it were not for the date 1852 carved on it, an ordinary observer would not see that it was modern.

Broughton must always have been a building of a domestic and peaceable character, but like many old houses of this period, there is a mysterious nook beginning in the cellar which passes at the back of the chimney in each storey to the attic, where probably there was a secret staircase much the same as the one that still exists at Emral. This staircase was intended as a means of escape in troublous times, while probably behind each chimney there was a place of concealment. I know of no evidence to tell the exact year when Broughton was built, and it is probable there was a house there previously. I think we may say we know that Randle Broughton, who married Margaret, daughter and heir of David, ap Ellis, of Eyton, Ruabon, lived there in 1500, and he was succeeded by Leland's John Broughton, who married Margaret, daughter of William Wiltan, Esq., who was succeeded by Randle Broughton, who married Jane, daughter of Roger Puleston, of Emral, Esq., who died 1572. Their son, John Broughton, married Susanna, daughter of Edward Bellof, of Moreton and Burton, Esq. He was an ardent supporter of King Charles I. and signed a protestation and oath that he would maintain and defend the King's Majesty and the just privileges of Parliament at a council holden at Salop, 1643 (Emral MS.). His wife Susanna was buried at Worthenbury, 2nd March, 1651; he also was buried there 4th February, 1655.

They had an only daughter Elizabeth, who was

married at Worthenbury, 11th June, 1650, to Roland Whitehall, of Lockwood, in the Parish of Kingsley, Staffordshire.

Elizabeth had three brothers, but they all died without issue. Her eldest brother was baptised and buried at Worthenbury, 1702; his wife, Mrs. Awdry Broughton, was buried in the same place in 1695. John and Thomas, brothers of Elizabeth, were two of the trustees for the house, tythe, corn, etc., settled by Judge Puleston on the ministers of Worthenbury, 1658. It must have been during the ownership of the elder of these brothers that Broughton was robbed by a thief "last week" as Philip Henry's diary shows, 1682, "and the thief taken and hanged."

Elizabeth's son, John Whitehall, was born the year of the restoration, 1660, and married Mary, daughter of Sir Andrew Hacket, of Moxhul, Warwickshire. Their son, Broughton Whitehall, married Letitia, daughter of Robert Davies, of Gwysaney, Flintshire and Llannerch, Denbighshire. (I have an interesting correspondence with John Whitehall and Thomas Puleston, of Emral, which I shall give later on). He was buried at Worthenbury, 22nd September, 1734, as also was his wife, December 18th, 1741. Of this marriage there were four daughters : Letitia married Robert Davies, 1734; Elizabeth married Peter Davies, who afterwards owned Broughton : Susanna married John Broughton Whitehall, died, 1762 ; Mary married Robert Dod, of Cloverley.

Letitia Davies, who was born at Broughton, 1735, inherited Llanerch, and left her property to her cousin, daughter and heiress of Peter Davies. She married Rev. George Allanson. Her name was Anne Elizabeth, and she was married at Worthenbury by Reginald Heber, of immortal fame, 1794. The Rev. Whitehall Whitehall Davies, who added much to Broughton Hall, died there, 1824, unmarried, and it was at his death Mrs. Allanson succeeded. She had five children, George Allanson, of Llanerch, died without issue ; Cuthbert died without issue ; Elizabeth married John Whitehall Dod, of Cloverley, at Worthenbury in 1822. Their son, Whitehall Dod, succeeded to the Llanerch property and died without issue, when it went with the Malpas property to the present Sir George Cayley, whose mother, Dorothy Allanson, was married at Worthenbury, 1830, to Digby Cayley.

It was John Whitehall Dod who sold Broughton
to its present owner, Mr. Robert Howard, 1852. Mr.
Whitehall Davies, as well as "old" Peter Davies, were
very well known and both highly respected. They
were the last sportsmen, I have been told, in England
or Wales, who netted partridges in the day time
as an amusement. I believe Whitehall Davies built
all the servants' offices and the stables at Broughton,
and made many inside structural alterations there.
He must have spent a great deal of money on the
house, which was charged on the property, and when
the corn laws were repealed in 1847, and there was
a consequent depression in agriculture, Mr. Dod
decided to sell it in consequence, as he told me, of
the incumbrances on it. Mrs. Allanson, however,
for her life succeeded her brother. She died August,
1841, and was buried at Worthenbury, aged seventy-
eight. I remember well being taken as a boy to see
her. She was sitting in one of the upper rooms looking
on the Ruabon hills, and very pretty she looked in
the bright sun, and kind, too, as she sent to the
gardens for some strawberries for me; they were the
small black sweet hautboys, which I have scarcely
ever tasted since.

Mr. John Whitehall Dod succeeded her, but as he owned Cloverley, he let Broughton to Mr. and Mrs. Isaac Hodgson, and very kind good neighbours they were ; but in a very few years they left and were succeeded by Lady Grey Egerton, widow of the Rev. Sir Philip Egerton, who occupied it with her son-in-law, Mr. Charles Cotton, and her daughter, until the present owner took possession in 1852. They were a great loss to the parish ; very charitable but very discriminating, personally examining into every case of distress, and her experience as a clergyman's widow was of great value to her neighbours. Charles Cotton farmed the home land, and ever seemed equally pleased with fine weather (good for the hay, he said) or wet—capital for turnips. All their children were I think born there, and one little boy of theirs lies in Worthenbury churchyard.

Broughton is situated on the Cheshire side of the parish, bounded on the north side by Shocklach and the east by Threapwood, which was formerly an extra parochial place ; it is on the line of one of the old Roman roads leading to Chester. Till 1817 Threapwood was dependent on Worthenbury for the offices of religion, as their children were usually baptised here and their funerals took place in this churchyard. Pennant derives Threapwood from the Anglo-Saxon Threapian—one who persisted in an argument right or wrong; and this derivation would apply to this district, as the inhabitants resisted all government and even the excise laws. Lord Hanmer, however, is of opinion that the name is from the Saxon word Threp, a ford, referring to one on the old road through the river Elf.

Archdeacon Thomas says, Threapwood is an ecclesiastical district, partly in Flintshire and partly in Cheshire, and was formed out of the old Domesday forest of Broughton, portions of which have been annexed to the parishes of Malpas and Worthenbury, comprising an area of about 240 acres as belonging to no parish. It had an unenviable notoriety as a refuge for immorality and lawlessness, but of this character it has now cleared itself. The population is, I think, 306; the church was built 1817.

The picture of the inner life of an agricultural labourer there at the close of the last century and the early years of this, as set before me by an old

man of eighty-five, some forty years ago, was a very
dismal one : "cock fighting, drinking, swearing, bull
baiting" were their pleasures.   In all of these my
old friend confessed, with something of a twinkle
in his eye, that he had joined ; but after nearly
exhausting the decalogue he added, " but nothing
worse."   In the early years of the last century there
was a scheme for joining Threapwood to the township of Cuddington, in the Parish of Malpas, which,
however, did not meet with the approval of this
parish, so that Mr. Kirk, who was then agent for
the Emral property, drew up a remonstrance, which
ran thus : " Some reasons offered by the inhabitants
of Worthenbury why that common called Threapwood should not be wholly annexed to the township
of Cuddington, in Cheshire.   1st.   Though it is
allowed that the aforesaid wood or common does
lie betwixt the two counties of Flint and Chester,
yet the boundaries of Flintshire side are of greater
extent than of the Cheshire side, and that part of
the wood or common that adjoins the township of
Worthenbury is near twice as much as what adjoins
to the township of Cuddington.   2nd.   Whereas
there is but one cottage and three tenements, none

exceeding £30 per annum on the Cheshire side of
the wood, and one of these in the township of
Cuddington, that have their riding or driving ways
to or over the said wood, there are on the Flintshire side seven houses inhabited by freeholders
and tenants, besides a gentleman's house and large
demesne that have no other way to either church
or market but upon and over the above named wood
and common. 3rd. There is a very great road
from Hanmer, 'Elesmere,' and Shrewsbury leading
to Chester, which is from one end of the said
common to the other, and upon this way, upon the
said common, are two bridges, one of two large
stone arches over the river Elf, the other of stone
and timber, both of which bridges were built and
constantly repaired at the sole charge of the inhabitants that are on the Flintshire side of the said
Threapwood, without any assistance of the township of Cuddington. And, further, as the freeholders
of the Parish of Worthenbury do hope to have their
rights and privileges to the Common of Threapwood continued to them and their heirs, so they
much desire that some effectual way may be found
to have the laws put into execution and that peace

may be kept and good order preserved there, as in other parts of His Majesty's dominions."

Lord Hanmer, in his memorial of the Parish of Hanmer, gives the following letters, which he says are in his possession, between Mr. Warburton, who at that time he believed was member for Chester, and Lord Chancellor Hardwicke,

"Chester, 4th August, 1753.

" My Lord,—It is by your Lordship's permission that I trouble you with the present state of a place called Threap Wood, or Common, lying between the counties of Chester and Flint, reputed to be in no county, parish, town, or hamlet. It contains about 300 acres, the greatest part of which is waste land, but very improvable; the rest is covered with seven-and-twenty cottages and small enclosures, and the inhabitants of these cottages were about two months ago numbered at one hundred and fifty. It is mostly encompassed by the parish of Worthenbury, Maelor Hundred, in the county of Flint; on the Cheshire side is the Parish of Malpas. I find this place mentioned in the Acts of Parliament for preparing soldiers in Queen 'Ann's' reign: certain persons being there assembled to avoid being prepared for

soldiers when Sir Joseph Jekyll, then Chief Justice
of Chester, obtained a clause that the Commissioners
for executing those Acts in the county of Chester
might have the like power in Threapwood. And as
I was apprehensive that the same inconvenience
might again happen, the like clause was obtained on
my motion in the House of Commons in a Press
Act which passed in the last Parliament. I do not
find this place mentioned in any other Act of
Parliament, law book, or case whatsoever, as the
cottages and inclosures in this place cannot be
assessed to the land tax in any county, neither do
the inhabitants pay any rates or tax whatsoever,
except the alesellers, who, by the assistance of the
Flintshire gentlemen, were brought under the duty
of beer and ale, and have paid that duty now about
twenty years. The right of common for cattle upon
the waste lands of this place has been constantly
and immemorially used by the inhabitants of the
several adjoining townships that lie in the counties
of Chester and Flint. As neither the Sheriffs of
Chester nor Flint were ever known to exercise their
office in this place, so no criminal or capital offence
committed in this place can be tried in either of

8

those counties, or anywhere else as I apprehend.*
The same inconvenience lies as to the jurisdiction of
Justices of the Peace.   And as there is no county
in which any ejectment can be brought, where can
the right, if there be any, to the cottages and
enclosures exist but in the present occupants ?   I
have heard that in former reigns, particularly in
King William's time, applications have been made to
the great seal by private persons for grants of this
place, no doubt with a view to enclose the whole and
render it private property.   But if ever there were
such grants, it is certain they were not submitted to,
and in all probability never will, by the inhabitants
of the several townships mentioned above, who have
time out of mind exercised their right of common
for cattle on this place.   It is, my Lord, because of
the obstruction to public justice, and that some
effectual way may be found out to have the laws put
into execution in this place, and that the peace may
be kept, and good order observed in Threapwood, as
in other parts of His Majesty's dominions, that

---

* Threapwood was commonly called the Holy Land on account
of this immunity.

reasons are found for submitting these facts to your Lordship's consideration, by

" Your most obedient and most humble servant,

" P. H. WARBURTON."

" Powis House, 21st August, 1753.

" Sir,—I should not have delayed so long to acknowledge the favour of your letter of the 4th inst., if my constant occupations during the continuance of my seals had not prevented me. I am extremely obliged to you for the particular account which you gave me of this extraordinary place Threapwood, the name whereof I have never heard before. But your mention of my old friend, Sir Joseph Jekyll, having first caused it to be inserted into the acts for preparing of soldiers in Queen Ann's wars, brought to my mind that I had heard him speak of a spot of ground in the country called ' Debateable Land.' Whether this be the same I cannot tell, but that I find that Skinner in his ' Etymologicon Linguæ Anglicanæ ' translates the word Threap or Threapen by the Latin word *redarguere*, which imports in some degree the sense of debate. The nature of the case speaks strongly that such a place must be the seat of much disorder and irregularity and the asylum of many disorderly persons to the interruption of justice, of which it is surprising that one has not heard more complaints. It is very laudable in you to have turned your thoughts to the redress of such an inconvenience, and I shall be very ready to co-operate in any proper measures for that purpose to the advancement of the public service, and to the satisfaction of the gentlemen of the country. I observe that in the clause which you procured to be inserted in the Act 18 Geo. II., this district is described as lying within or near the counties of Chester and Flint, or one of them, which induces me to conjecture that it may be claimed by both counties. I never heard of any application for a grant of this ground, nor do I believe that such grant ever passed. But if any such application ever was made, it must have been through the Treasury, for the Great Seal could have nothing to do with it except in the last stage by sealing letters patent. As we are now at so great a distance, I have desired Mr. Noel, your chief justice, to take an opportunity of conferring with you on this subject, to which I presumed you would have no objection, as the affair concerns the public service.

"I am, with much respect, Sir,

"Your most obedient humble servant,

"HARDWICKE."

Incredible as it may appear, Threapwood formerly had its race meeting, which was supported by gentlemen of high position, among whom were Lord Molineux, Sir Robert Grosvenor, Sir John Glynn, Sir Robert Cotton, Sir William Williams, Sir Rowland Hill, W. Williams Wynn, John Myddleton, Robert Pigott, of Chetwyn, Edward Mainwaring, Thomas Lloyd, Robert Williams, Arthur Owen, Broughton Whitehall, Thomas Ravenscroft, Cawley Humberston, Thomas Whitby, Col. Handersyd, Edward Williams, Nerquis, George Shackerley, Thomas Mostyn, Edward Williams, of Ysten, Colwyn, Robert Price, and Thomas Puleston, Esqs.; all of whom subscribed a guinea. They ran for a purse, value twenty-five guineas, each starter paid £2 2s., and they were started by a trumpeter who had a fee of five shillings. The articles of running are in Mr. Kirk's handwriting, agent to Mr. Thomas Puleston.

I own two pictures of horses in training, which no doubt ran at this and kindred meetings at Tilstone and elsewhere. They are nearer the style of the present hunter than the modern racehorse. No doubt, however, these races created some excitement in the neighbourhood, and were witnessed by a fashionable gathering; in that day, about 165 years ago, when London and Paris were not close to us, as they are now by the help of steam.

Canon Lee remarks on the number of moated houses there were in this vicinity. Halghton Hall, formerly owned by the Lloyds, is one of these. There was also one at Penley Hall, but not on the site of the present house; it stood inside the old garden. The moat is fairly perfect now, but when this house was pulled down I know not. There was another opposite Talarn Green, belonging to the Lloyds, Tal y wern, and called by the villagers, the Hall of Talents. Subsequently it belonged to the Phillips's, of Horseman's Green.

James Clark, a labourer in this parish twenty years ago or more, said he helped to fill in the moat, and was wont to tell how the last owner clung to his chimneycorner when his lands were gone and the old hall in ruins. A lane called the Coach Road still keeps in memory the home of a gentle family of bygone days.

In Worthenbury there are in all three moated houses. At the Holly or Holy Bush Farm, there is a small but clearly defined moat; unfortunately, nothing whatever is known of the old house that stood inside it or the history of those who lived in it. The present farm-house is a mixture of recent work and some probably of the middle of the last century, but leaning against this there is a very curious buttress, which is without doubt very old, and may have been a part of the old house, which must have been of far greater size than the present house. I have, however, not been able to find out anything relating to it among the Emral papers. It would be to me most interesting if something should come to light to give us the history of this old relic.

At Mulsford Hall, there is an unmistakeable moat on the western side, and there are indications, too, that this house was of some importance. It was situated on the branch Roman road passing by Emral to Bangor; but here the same difficulty arises, and there is a singular absence of all history or tradition of the moated house or the dwellers in it. Even the names of the very old tenants are unknown, except that of " Mr. Phillips, gentleman," who lived there in the days of the Commonwealth. We do know, however, by a stone let into the wall with the following inscription on it, that " This house was built by C. Matthews, tenant to John Puleston, Esq. 'Tis for my landlord's good and my own desire. 1746." The house is built of red brick, and both bricks and workmanship bear evidence that the same hands made the bricks and put them together as built Worthenbury Church and the wings of Emral House. It was in this house that the Messrs. Parry lived and died of whom mention has already been made. The Bootes, also a very well known family, lived here, but before my time. It was probably from clay taken from the field called Brick Kiln Field that the bricks for the present house, Emral wings, and Worthenbury Church were made.

The third moated house in the parish is Emral Hall, which, as I have already told, was the dower house of Emma Audley, widow of the owner of Castle Dinas Brân. Her husband, as Prince of Powys, owned all this country

for miles, up to Broxton Hills, including Fenns
Wood, but in those early days a woman, especially
one advanced in life, could scarcely hold her own,
so that we find that she was soon dispossessed of
her property, when it was granted by King Edward
I. to Roger de Puleston. The Pulestons came over
with the Conqueror, and settled in Shropshire, and
exercised great influence on the Welsh border in the
13th century. Edward I. then had a great work
before him in Wales, and he knew that he could
trust Roger Puleston to do it. No doubt it was on
this account that he granted it to him in preference
to Richard Puleston, to whom it was first given, as
from Emral he could soon be in Wales to keep the
Welsh in order.

Emral is said to have been built for Emma
Audley in 1272, but it seems scarcely possible
for any part of the present house to have been
built as early as that time, and yet with all the
mass of Emral papers in my possession I cannot
find any bills for building at Emral before the middle
of the last century, but I think it is nearly impossible
that there could have been any considerable building
done there since 1500, except what I shall tell of in

the last century, without my coming across some account of it in the Emral MSS.

In very early days there were without doubt a good many armed retainers kept at Emral, not only to protect the place, but for the King's service, and it was probably on this account that there was a chapel at Emral, as the troopers would not be allowed to go as far as Worthenbury or Bangor church, and so leave the house unprotected: and as late as the time of the Civil War we know that there were a good many troops in occupation of it, first on behalf of King Charles I., then of Oliver Cromwell. It would be most interesting to know where these troops lived. Canon Lee says there was a tower on the north side of Emral; if so, it must have been joined on to the present moat. If there was this tower it may have been devoted to their use. This tower in that case would protect the north front, while the present moat, if it extended on the south side and joined the brook with a drawbridge over it, and perhaps another where the back entrance to the house now is, would make the house secure, if it were carefully watched, though only so long as no cannon were used. But I shall have to write, as nearly as I can make out, what happened there when I come to the time of the Civil War.

Judge Puleston, who plays the most prominent part in the history of this parish in the time of the Parliamentary struggle, succeeded his cousin Sir Roger Puleston at Emral, after a short occupation by the widow of this Sir Roger, who, as well as his brother George, died without children. His father, Richard Puleston, was the fourth son of Roger Puleston and Anne Grosvenor. To get to this time I have to pass over a great many Pulestons, simply because I only know their names and who they married, and where they and their children were married, baptized, and buried; but I cannot tell you what part they played in the history of this parish.

Judge Puleston being a younger son, and having good ability, studied for the bar and became in process of time a Serjeant-at-Law, and Chief Justice of the Common Pleas, as well as Chief Justice of Lancashire. The Sir Roger whom he succeeded was on the side of Parliament, and took as his motto, "*Pro Deo et Republicâ*" and so also was the Judge, though his kinsmen the Hanmers and his neighbours the Broughtons were on the side of Charles I. He

does not appear, however, to have taken an active
part in the war, yet his house Emral was seized
several times by the adherents of the King and
Parliament, and at the hands of the former he suffered
a heavy pecuniary loss, as the following petition
shows :—

"To the Honourable Committee of Parliament

at Goldsmith's Hall.

"The humble petition of John Puleston, of the
Middle Temple, Esquire, shewing that Sir Thomas
Hanmer, Baronet, in the year 1642, by colour of
some grant from the King, did enter upon your
Petitioner's houses, lands, and tenements in the
counties of Flint and 'Denby,' and hath ever since
taken and converted to his own use the Petitioner's
goods, 'chattles,' and rents to the value of £6000,
and at this time with troopers and others, his agents,
doth gather this Petitioner's rents from his tenants;
that with much cruelty and 'barberousness' the said
Hanmer drove the Petitioner's young children, sucking
their nurse's breast, out of the Petitioner's houses to
be fostered by the charity of the people. And now,
notwithstanding he is still in actual arms in Wales

against Parliament, is endeavouring to make his composition with this Honourable Committee.

" The Petitioner, therefore, humbly beseecheth this Honourable Committee that if they shall conceive this man, being the chief ringleader of the Welsh rebels, to be incapable of any composition with this Honourable Committee, that then there may be a special saving of the Justice of the two Houses of Parliament for this Petitioner's losses out of the said Sir Thomas Hanmer's estate.

" And your Petitioner will ever pray, etc."

Sir Thomas Hanmer replies to this that he saved John Puleston's wood from being cut down and sold; that Emral was garrisoned first by Captain Ratcliffe, next by Major St. John, and then by Captain David Morris; that Captain Ratcliffe was a stranger in the country, and that he made havoc of his goods, and that he, Sir Thomas, had done his best to save what he could from being carried away. In what way this matter was settled there are no papers in my possession to show, but Judge Puleston seems to have been somewhat worsted, as his son, afterwards Sir Roger Puleston, was a staunch Royalist, and the Parliamentary party when victorious were down upon him, so that father and son suffered money losses, all of which must have come out of the Judge's pocket.

The Parliamentary troops retook Emral, and they also took Hanmer House, where Sir Thomas Hanmer lived. The account of their taking them is as follows: " When they saw the piece of ordnance we had, they yielded both houses, allowing the troops to march away without their arms : their captain and ensign to remain prisoners." Emral was then garrisoned by Cromwell's men, but what their numbers were I know not, but in March, 1644, " forty horse and forty muskiteers being left behind them," the remainder issued out, intending to have taken the enemy in their quarters at Farn, but they had notice of their coming, and so they found the " Town empty," but presently returned and took all the foot and four of the horses, with their arms.

These would be stirring times for Worthenbury, and no doubt the village inn would nightly be crowded by the inhabitants and troopers who went there, in the absence of a daily paper, to learn the latest intelligence. Judge Puleston married a most excellent lady, Elizabeth, daughter of Thomas Wolrych, Esq., of Dudmaston, and sister of Sir Francis Wolrych ; her mother was a sister of Susanna, wife of Sir Roger Puleston, of Emral.   This marriage is in our parish register, 21st December, 1635, though possibly the marriage did not take place here.   The entry runs thus : " Johannes Puleston armiger et Elizabeth Wolrych."

In 1653 Judge Puleston was fortunate enough to secure an excellent young man from Oxford, " to take the oversight of his sons until they were ready for the University, and to preach at Worthenbury on the Lord's day."   This was Philip Henry, whose name is still remembered in the parish with veneration.   The Judge's wife writes to her cousin, Mr. Palmer, who recommended Philip Henry, that she is so satisfied with what he proposed " that there needs no further trouble ; " she adds, " I have delivered the bearer £5 for the gentleman in part of the first quarter; what the charge for the journey takes out of it I will supply at the quarter's end, when I pay the rest to make out £15.   I have sent a horse and a footman to wait on him hither." Philip Henry thus records his coming to Emral 30th September, 1653 : " By the means of Mr. Francis

Palmer, I came to Emrall in Flintshire to teach his sons and to preach at Worthenbury. The Lord bee with me there." Philip Henry was brought up at Whitehall. It seems only natural, being so very near, that he should have gone to Westminster School, which he did, and was put in the fourth form under Mr. Thomas Vincent, whom he describes as the most diligent schoolmaster he ever knew. While there he attended the services at Westminster Abbey and St. Margarets, which was their Parish Church. In May, 1647, he was chosen to Oxford with four others ; of these he had the second place. " The December following I went to Oxford, lay the first night in my journey at Maidenhead, where, being a young traveller, never so far before on horseback, and riding hard for company's sake, I swooned, and was much made of, though by strangers. The next day parting with them at Dorchester, whence six or seven miles to Oxford, I was much concerned that I must ride so far alone, and not knowing what to do, it pleased God so to order it for me that at the townes-end I overtook Mr. Annesley and his man whom I missed of at my setting forth from London, and had their company, which I then and often since looked upon as a great mercy, though in a small matter."

At the end of 1648-9 he tells us, " I went to London to see my father, and during my stay there at that time at Whitehall it was that I saw the beheading of King Charles I. On the day of his execution, which was Tuesday, 30th January, I stood amongst the crowd in the street before Whitehall Gate, where the scaffold was erected, and saw what was done, but not so as to hear anything. The blow I saw given, and can truly say with a sad heart, at the instant whereof, I remember wel, there was such a grone by the thousands then present as I never heard before, and desire I may never hear again. There was, according to order, one troop immediately march-ing from-wards Charing Cross to Westminster, and another from-wards Westminster to Charing Cross, purposely to masker the people and to disperse and scatter them, so that I had much adoe among the rest to escape home without hurt."

It was the 9th January, 1653, that he preached his first sermon at Hincsey, in Oxfordshire, John viii. 34 v. This was the same year he went to Emral. The beheading of the King must have been a real sorrow

9

to Philip Henry, as he was known personally to the King, as he had been a playmate and a great favourite with the young princes. For many years he observed the 30th January as a day of humiliation. In religion Philip Henry loved " the large Gospel and strict religion of the Commonwealth," and was a sincere and hearty Puritan ; so though without doubt his heart was sad at the death of the King, yet his sympathies were with the Commonwealth party. When he came to Emral he was only twenty-two ; and he only undertook the work for six months, " provided that he might be required to preach but once on the Lord's day." We find he prayed in the family, was tutor to Judge Puleston's five sons, and preached once a day at Worthenbury.

The Church was said to have been a chapelry under Bangor, but, since the rebellion, it had been used very sparingly, and I find that our parish registers had been most irregularly kept, though there are a few entries in them at this time. Philip Henry kept the registers most neatly, and the entries he made are as legible as the day he wrote them, more than two hundred years ago. At the end of the stipulated six months Philip Henry returned to

Oxford, whither in June, 1654, Lady Puleston followed him with her five sons, "the two eldest under my charge in the colledge." His preaching at Worthenbury had been blessed with the happiest results, as the following letter of Lady Puleston shows: "This I am sure, that having wanted hitherto a good minister of the Word amongst us I have oft, by prayers and some tears, about five years besought God for such a one as yourself, which having obtained, I cannot yet despair, seeing He has given us the good means, but He may also give us the good end. And this I find, that your audience hath increased three for one in the parish, though in winter, more than formerly in summer; and five for one out of other places. And I have neither heard of their being in the ale house on the Lord's day, nor ball playing, which before you came was frequent. I think I can name four or five in the parish, that of formal Christians are become or becoming real; but you know all are not wrought on at first by the Word: God may call them at the latter part of the day, though not in this half year. It is good sign that most are loath to part with you, and you have done more good in this half year than I have discerned these eighteen years; but, however, whether they will hear or whether they will forbear, you have delivered your own soul. I have prayed and do pray, seeing God sent you, that you may be for His glory and not for our condemnation."

During his visit to London during his next vacation, he received a letter from Judge Puleston with a very solemn affectionate request subscribed by the parishoners of Worthenbury, earnestly desiring his settlement among them as their minister, and this led to his entering on the charge in the winter of 1654. The Pulestons claimed from time immemorial the advowson of Worthenbury, the tithe of which belonged to them, but Mr. Thomas Lloyd, of Halghton, who was then the owner of the advowson of Bangor, and had a sort of claim, through Emral Chapel being served from Bangor, renounced and gave up to the Judge any claim he had to the patronage of Worthenbury, and then Bangor and Worthenbury were separated. At the restoration, however, this arrangement was repudiated, and the separation of the two parishes was not finally completed until the second year of William and Mary. We find a great deal of

correspondence on the subject, of which the following is of interest :—

"The case concerning the Parish Church and
Chapelry of Emral is thus truly stated :

" Judge Puleston, Sergeant-at-Law, is seised of an
ancient mansion house called Emerall, within the
Parish of Worthenbury, and that he and all those
whose estate he hath in the said mansion house have
for all time whereof the memory of man is not to
the contrary, collated a fit parson to the said church,
and that the parson so collated have for all the time
aforesaid received and enjoyed all the tithe hay and
all other small tithes yearly growing within the
bounds and precincts of the said parish, the value of
which is not much more than £20 per annum.
There is likewise within the said parish an ancient
chapel belonging to the said mansion house of
Emerall, which chapel is annexed to the parson of
Bangor, and that for time out of mind the said parson
has received £20 per annum from the said John
Puleston and his predecessors for the tithe corn of
the Parish of Worthenbury, and for the performing
of Divine service in the said chapel, which service
the incumbent never performed. The Parsonage of

Bangor is worth £200 per annum, and hath annexed to it the Parish Church of Owton, worth £120 per annum. The desire of the said Mr. Puleston is that the said chapelry might be re-united to the Parish Church of Worthenbury, out of which it was taken, and that the tithes worth [torn out] may be granted and united to the parson of the Parish Church of Worthenbury and his successors, and that £20 formerly paid to the Parish of Bangor may be extinguished, and that a certain close called the Boate or [torn out] in Worthenbury being the inheritance of the said John Puleston, may likewise be settled to the parson of the said Parish Church of Worthenbury and his successors for ever, upon which the said John Puleston intends to build all necessary houses for the accommodation of the said parson and his successors.

"JOHN PULESTON.

"It appears from Emral deeds that the sheriff of Flint, Ra Hughes., Esq., 1657, was required by the ecclesiastical commission appointed by the High Court of Chancery to call a jury to consider the case of Bangor Parish and the chapels attached to it to meet on the 19th April, 1657, at the house of Robert ap Richard, in Bangor, at the hour of 8 o'clock in the morning.

              " Signed by

                " JOHN BROUGHTON.

                " OWEN BARTON.

                " RICHARD BISNETT.

" Mr. Lloyd.   " ROGER PULESTON.

" The Jurors on their oath say that the Parish of Worthenbury, in the county of Flint, is a parish church to which the cure of souls is annexed, and that John Puleston, Sergeant-at-Law, is seised in his demesne as of fee of an ancient messuage called Emerall, in Worthenbury, in the county of Flint, and of divers lands, meadows, and pastures therein belonging, and that the said John and all those whose estate he hath in the ———— by all the time wherein the memory of man is not to the contrary, have collated as clerk to the said Parish Church of Worthenbury, as oft as the said became void (except in the time of the late Lady Puleston's widowhood, who held the said house of Emerall during her life), and they likewise say that the clerks so collated by all the time aforesaid, have or ought to have enjoyed the tithe hay arising within the said Parish of

Worthenbury, and all the tithe wool, lambs, and other small tithes arising within the said parish or a composition for the same, which tithes are worth £20 by the year.

" They further say that Philip Henry, Master of Arts, a learned and diligent preacher of the Gospel, is minister and incumbent of the Church of Worthenbury by the collation of the said John Puleston. They further find that in the said Parish of Worthenbury there is, and by all the time whereof the memory of man is not to the contrary, hath been an ancient chapel annexed to the Parish Church of Bangor, and that the said John Puleston and all those whose estate he hath in the said estate and messuage of Emerall and premises, have had and enjoyed the tithe corn yearly growing within the said Parish of Worthenbury, paying yearly for the same £20 to the parsons of Bangor for the time being, as in right of the said chapel, the said tithes being ordinarily worth £60 by the year.

" They likewise found that Mr. Henry Bridgman is parson of Bangor, and that Robert Ffogg, clerk, doth serve the cure and take the tithes of Bangor to his own use by sequestration for the delinquency of

Mr. Henry Bridgman. They find that the tithes of Bangor are worth £150 by the year. They find that the church of Worthenbury and the chapel in Worthenbury are distant two miles from the church of Bangor, and the chapel in Worthenbury is distant from the parish church about one mile.

" They likewise say that the chapel in Worthenbury hath cure of souls, and that the parsons of Bangor, for ought that they can find, have not performed any Divine service there.

" They also find that Sir Thomas Hanmer, Bart., and Thomas Lloyd, Esq., are patrons of the church of Bangor and the chapel in Worthenbury thereto annexed, and that John Puleston, Sergeant-at-Law, is patron of the Donative Church of Worthenbury, and the said Jurors further say that they hold it fit that the said chapel in Worthenbury and the said pension of £20 by the year should be severed and taken from the said Parsonage of Bangor and be settled to the Parish Church of Worthenbury, in the same manner as they are now settled and annexed to Bangor, and the said Jurors say that they do not know of any spiritual or ecclesiastical benefice, living and donative, with or without a cure of souls, within the said parish of Bangor or the limits thereof, neither have they any evidence given them of any other ecclesiastical benefices."

From Lady Puleston to Dr. Owen, Dean of Christ Church, Oxford.

" My much Honoured Cosin,—I was in hopes that I should have seen you here as you purposed last spring and am very sorry it fell out otherwise; it hath pleased the Lord to lay me low under His hand by much payn, and many months sickness from a cancer in my breast, and I am waiting every day till my change cometh, but if we meet no more on earth I hope wee shall in the armes of Jesus Christ. There is a friend of mine whose name is Edward Thomas, of Wrexham, who brings his son to your colledge and I request you to countenance him with your favour; the youth is very hopefull, both in learning and in grace, and his father, an ancient professor of Godliness in these parts and one of approved integrity and, I know, Sir, that such and what concernes them lyes near your heart upon far greater and better interests than mine, and I persuade my selfe what your opportunities will permitt you to doe in his behalfe, you will receive a full recompense

of reward for, from Him who hath promised to re-
quite even a cup of cold water given in the name of a
disciple. Mr. H. is here with me. What my husband
intends concerning him is not yet settled, but I hope
shortly it will bee, in the meantime I am loth hee
should leave a certainty in the colledge for an
uncertainty here, and doe therefore desire you to
continue his place to him for a while longer, that,
seeing the Lord hath made him willing to lay him-
selfe in the work of the Gospel so far remote from
his friends in this poor dark corner of the land, hee
may not in anything bee prejudiced for our sakes.
My husband is at London or in his way home, wee
and ours are much engaged to you for your love, and
I should have been very glad if it might have fallen
within the compasse of my abilityes to make known
other 'then' by words my sense of your many
kindnesses, but, 'tis the Lord's will that I should
dye your debtor; with my true unfayned respects
and service to your lady and selfe,

"I rest, Your affectionate Cosin and Friend,

"E. P."

This gives us an insight into the sacrifice Philip
Henry was making by giving up his career at Oxford

for such work as he found at Emral and Worthenbury. From this letter we see how intimately
connected the Parishes of Bangor and Worthenbury
have been since the Christian religion was first
received by our forefathers, and it is on this account
that I have written so much of the History of
Bangor from the earliest times.

Judge Puleston was especially anxious to keep Philip
Henry as minister of Worthenbury and to effect this he
was willing to give up the tithe, clear of the charge to
the Rector of Bangor to the ministers of Worthenbury
for ever, but in order to avoid the difficulty of collecting the tithes in those very unsettled times and
to show his especial regard for Philip Henry, he
gave a deed of indenture bearing date 6th October,
1655, settling upon him the yearly rent of £100
charged upon all his property in the counties of
Flint, Denbigh, and Chester to be paid quarterly
until such times as the said Philip Henry should be
promoted to some other ecclesiastical preferment,
with power of distress in case of non-payment.

Philip Henry remained for about two years an
inmate of the Judge's family at Emral, though he
complains that he found there snares and tempta-

tions which seem to have arisen because some of the
Puleston family did not resemble their parents and
were uneasy at his presence among them. The
judge saw this very plainly, and to avoid any
further unpleasantness in his family circle, built at
his own charge " a handsome brick house and settled
him there by deed, dated 5th March, 1657, for sixty
years if he should so long continue minister of
Worthenbury. The foundations of this house were
laid in August and the house finished 12th November,
1657, at a cost of £800 " (Emral MSS.). So this
shows that the house Judge Puleston built for Philip
Henry cost nearly as large a sum as was the esti-
mated cost of Worthenbury New Church, though
this was nearly a century later.

In 1658, supplementing the deed of settlement
above mentioned there is another deed (in the parish
chest) which confirms more extensive benefits to
the ministers of Worthenbury. The deed is as
follows:—

" This indenture made the 29th July, 1658, between
John Puleston, of Emerall, in the county of Flint,
Sergeant-at-Law, of the one part and John Brough-
ton, of Broughton, in the said county of Flint, Esq.,

Thomas Puleston, of Emerall, aforesaid, one of the sons of the said John Puleston, and Edward, another of the sons of the said John Puleston, Thomas Broughton, of Broughton, aforesaid, brother of John Broughton, Roger Puleston, of Worthenbury, Gent., Edward Phillips, of Mulsford, Gent., John Holliman, of Worthenbury, Gent., and Griffith Jones, of the same, yeoman, of the other part, witnesseth that the said John Puleston, for the settling of the house in Worthenbury, newly built with brick, the croft where-on it stands and the land and lane leading to it from Emerall mills to Griffith Jones, his house and all the tythe corn yearlie renewing and growing in Worthen-bury aforesaid, for the better maintenance of a preacher in the said parish, hath given, granted, and enfeoffed and confirmed unto the said John Broughton, Thomas Puleston, etc., all his new brick house afore-said, the croft whereon it stands, etc., unto the said John Broughton, etc., and their heirs for ever upon this speciall trust and confidence that they shall permitt and suffer the minister of Worthenbury for the tyme being to have and enjoy the said house for ever, etc. In witness, whereof, the parties above

named have unto these presents interchanged their
hands and seals.

"JOHN PULESTON.

"DAVID ROCHE, Dr. of Physique.

"PHILIP HENRY, Minister.

"ROBERT BICKLEY."

Philip Henry was now anxious, and indeed made
arrangements that his long deferred ordination
should take place at Worthenbury in the presence
of his people, but the ministers were unwilling to
set such a precedent. The Presbytery by which
he was ordained was in the Hundred of Bradford
North, in Shropshire. The members of this class,
which was authorised by an ordinance of both Houses
of Parliament 29th August, 1648, for the ordination
of ministers, were Mr. Porter, of Whitechurch,
Boughey, of Hodnet, Houghton, of Prees, Parsons,
of Wem, etc.

In July, 1657, he submitted to examination at
Prees. On the Sunday before ordination a notice
was read in the church at Worthenbury, and afterwards affixed to the church door : "That if anyone could produce any just exceptions against the
doctrine or life of Philip Henry, or any sufficient

reason why he might not be ordained, they should certify the same to the Classis, and it should be heard and considered." Having previously made his profession of the Presbyterian faith, the Presbyters laid their hands on him with words to this effect, " Whom we do thus in Thy name set apart to the work and office of the ministry." This took place 16th September, 1657.

In the year 1659 Mr. Henry was collated and presented to the church of Worthenbury by Judge Puleston. Mr. Ffogg, who had displaced Mr. Henry Bridgman, and was then Rector of Bangor, opposed this arrangement as entrenching on his rights, therefore Philip Henry was anxious that the Judge should give him reasonable satisfaction, while he himself put in writing that he desired Mr. Ffogg's consent that he should be minister of Worthenbury. This seems to have been deemed sufficient, and for the future they were firm friends. For eight years Philip Henry continued his work at Worthenbury, where he was much loved, and gained the name of the " Heavenly Henry." The death of Lady Puleston, September 29th, 1658, was a sad blow to him. She was a thoroughly pious woman, but, I fear, had a painful end from cancer. She had been long a fast friend of Philip Henry's, and he had much comfort from the countenance and conversation of her, as well as of the Judge. He says of her, " She was the best friend I ever had on earth, but my Friend in heaven is still where He was and will never leave nor forsake me." He preached her funeral sermon from Isa. xi. 22. Her last prayer was " My soul leans to Jesus Christ, lean to me, sweet Saviour."

About this time he writes : " A dark cloud is over my life in this family, but my desire is that what-soever becomes of me and my interest, the interest of Christ may still be kept on foot in this place. Amen, so be it."

Our parish register says : " Elizabeth, the wife of Judge Puleston, of Emerall, was buryed the 7th October, 1658." Matthew Henry, in his biography of his father says she was " of more than ordinary parts and wisdom, in piety inferior to few, but in learning superior to most of her sex, which I could give instances of from what I find among Mr. Henry's papers, particularly an elegy she made on the death of the learned Mr. Seldon, who was her

10

great friend." Judge Puleston did not long survive his excellent wife ; Worthenbury Register says, "The Honble. John Puleston, of Emerall, was buryed 8th September, 1659." He died on the 5th, and Philip Henry preached his funeral sermon from Neh. xiii. 14.

The design of the sermon was not to applaud his deceased friend, but to show from instances of so great a benefactor to the ministry as the Judge had been, that deeds done for the house of God and the officers thereof are good deeds, and to press people to do the same according to their ability. Mr. Henry's interest and friendship with the Puleston family was now at an end. He and the Judge's successor never could get on together. Indeed, on one occasion Philip Henry records that " Roger Puleston assaulted mee in wrath, whereby my unruly passions being stirred, I strook again and hurt his face." In politics, which at this time caused great dissentions among friends and kins-folk, as well as in religion, they were diametrically opposed, and now at the restoration of Charles II. the Royalists, who no doubt had suffered greatly under the Commonwealth, were by no means particularly careful to avoid showing their dislike to the Roundheads. Philip Henry was, however, most desirous of carrying on the good work he was doing at Worthenbury, and declined the living of Wrexham and another near London.

Early in this year (1660) he married the only child of Mr. Matthews, of the Broad Oak, near Whitchurch. He soon was made to feel that he would be ejected from Worthenbury, as his conscience would not allow him to do all that was required of those clergymen who had been appointed to livings under the Parliamentary Ordinance of 1648, as he had been. He took, however, the oath of allegiance to King Charles II., but, though most moderate in his opinions, he would not consent to be re-ordained, neither would he assent to everything in the book of common prayer.

When the King was restored, Worthenbury reverted to Bangor and Dr. Bridgman, who had himself been restored to Bangor, incited by the Puleston family, formally ejected Philip Henry from his cure, October, 1661, the necessary papers being read in the church by one of the Puleston servants. He preached his farewell sermon the same afternoon from Ph. i. 27. Dr. Bridgman entered into an agreement with the Puleston's that the tithe of Worthenbury should be his from the day on which he should discharge Philip Henry and undertake never to re-admit him. Mr. Hilton was appointed in his place. For a few years Philip Henry remained at Worthenbury after his ejection, but he never preached there again, though he attended the church.

His annuity from Emral which was conferred upon him by Judge Puleston being withheld, he was advised to enter an action for its recovery, which at length he did; but for the sake of peace he consented to receive one hundred pounds and to give up the bond and the house, and thus he lost the benefit of Judge Puleston's great kindness to him. On the completion of this business in September, 1662, he left Worthenbury and went to live at Broad Oak, near Whitchurch. His connection with Worthenbury was never renewed, but after the lapse of more than two centuries his memory is still honoured.

Sir Roger Puleston, who seems to have treated Philip Henry so unworthily, was only twenty-two years of age when his father died. He was, moreover, as I have said, a staunch supporter of Royalty, for

which he was summoned before the Parliamentary
Commissioners for being in arms with Sir George
Boothe and his party in the late rebellion against the
Parliament and Commonwealth ; so that both in
politics and in religion he was opposed to his old
tutor.   As soon as he was established at Emral in
his father's room, he left no stone unturned to eject
Philip Henry.   He married a daughter of Roger
Mostyn, of Mostyn Hall, Flintshire.

This Sir Roger lived only for a very few years to
enjoy his position, but died 13th July, 1667, and was
buried in a chapel of the Old Parish Church at
Gresford, which then belonged to the Pulestons.
His widow, however, continued to reside at Emral
as guardian of her son, who was only four years old
when his father died.   In two years time she married
Sir John Trevor, who had been speaker of the House
of Commons, and they lived together at Emral, at
all events until 1683, as Philip Henry's diary records
that he took to Lady Trevor, at Emral, a silver cup
and patten, which Lady Puleston (the Judge's wife)
gave him to be disposed of as he should think fit.
He says he intended it for Worthenbury but his
removal prevented it being thus bestowed.   He says,

he waited on Sir John Trevor, at Emral, dined with him, and had a deal of discourse with him, both on public and private affairs. One naturally wonders what has become of this most valuable communion plate; there is, however, no use in lamenting the loss as I fear we shall now never see it in Worthenbury Church.

Sir John and Lady Trevor probably left Emral when her son Roger came of age. She had a jointure of seven hundred pounds per annum from Shocklach, which was paid her until 1704 when she died. Her son was knighted when he was only twenty years of age, and the fees he paid on the occasion are named in the Emral papers in my possession and are so curious that I venture to give the items :—

" A bill of ffees due to the king's servants from all persons that receave the honour of Knighthood due to them by virtue of a pattent granted under the great seale of England.

	£	s.	d.
" To the Earl Marshall of England ...	03	03	04
" To the King's Herald and persevants at arms	08	10	

	£	s.	d.
" To the Gentlemen ushers daily waiters	05	00	00
" To the Grooms of the Privy Chamber	05	00	00
" To the Gentlemen ushers quarter waiters	04	00	00
" To the Knight Harbinger	03	06	08
" To the Pages of the Bedchamber	04	00	00
" To the Roabes Office ...	04	00	00
" To the King's barbers	01	00	00
" To the Sergeant at arms ...	05	00	00
" To the Wardrobe office	02	05	04
" To the Sewers of your Chamber ...	02	00	00
" To the Gentlemen of your cellar and buttery	01	12	00
" To the Gentlemen and Yeomen Harbingers ...	05	06	08
" To the Sergeant Porter	01	00	00
" To the Porters at your gate... ...	01	00	00
" To the Closet Keeper	00	01	00
" To the Groom of the Chamber ...	01	00	00
" To the Yeoman Ushers	01	00	00
" To the Yeoman of the month ...	01	16	00
" To the Pages of your presence ...	00	10	00
" To the Surveyor of your wages ...	00	10	00
" To the Surveyor of your Dressing Chamber	00	10	00

	£	s.	d.

" To the Drum Major 00 10 00

" To the Sergeant of your trumpetts ... 03 00 00

" To the Footmen 02 00 00

" To the Coachman 00 10 00

" To the Corporals of the Guard of the

    King's body 05 00 00

" A further payment of £3, and some small items, makes the whole £81 13 4, for which a receipt is given :—

" ' Received of Sir Roger Puleston, Knight, by order of Mr. Ellis Lloyd, £81 13 4, being the severall fees due to the King's servants for " his " honor of Knighthood.

        " ' (Signed) 20th March, 1681-2,

    " ' THOMAS DUPPA, Gent. Usher Coll.' "

What the fees for this honour now amount to I cannot say, but I may mention here, just to show the difference in the purchasing power of money at this period with our day, that I find amongst the Emral papers a butcher's bill :—

	s.	d.

" One breast of veale and one quarter of

    lambe 1 9

    " Do. and calf's head ... 1 9

	s.	d.
" A quarter and shoulder of mutton	2	2
" Do.	0	7
" A leg of pork	2	4
" A loin of veale	1	0
" Two quarters of mutton	2	8
" A breast of beefe	3	4 "

As Sir Roger Puleston was so young when he was Knighted there is little doubt the honour was conferred upon him as a recognition of the service of his father to the cause of the King.

1683. Sir Roger, being desirous of carrying out the intentions of his grandfather Judge Puleston, declares his readiness to give up the tithe of Worthenbury to the parson thereof, "so as the said Parochial Chapel and Church of Worthenbury and all the townships, messuages, lands, and tythes within its known limits be for ever severed and separated from the Parish and Rectory of Bangor, and have a distinct rector, to be presentable for ever by the said Sir Roger Puleston and his heirs. With the consent of John, Bishop of Chester, and Thomas Lloyd, Esq., this arrangement was, after some correspondence, carried out in 1683, and the Act of Parliament confirming the same was passed in 1689.

This Sir Roger died of fever in London, February 28th, 1697, and by a wish expressed in his will, was buried in the Puleston Chapel at Gresford, he desired that his funeral expenses should not exceed £200, that his son should be educated at Eton school from ten to seventeen, and that then he should be sent to the University at Oxford until nineteen, and that then he should be entered at the Inner Temple. His widow was to have Emral rent free till his son came of age, and to her he left his coach and six! which shows us something of the state of the roads at that time.

From the accounts amongst the Emral papers I find Emral was repaired during this boy's minority. Ultimately, however, she left Emral because she found it too large for her, and an inventory was taken of the furniture, which is curious, but scarcely of sufficient interest to insert here.

Sir Roger's son Thomas was not three years old at his father's death, when he succeeded to the property and went to Eton, Oxford, and the Inner Temple, as his father's will appointed. I fear his expenditure was on somewhat of a magnificent scale, and he had to get two Acts of Parliament passed to enable him to sell property at Willington, Shocklach, and Gresford, besides selling a property lying close up to the Iron Gates of Chirk Castle. I have the inventory of furniture, plate, cattle, etc. that Sir Roger had at Plas Newydd Chirk at his death.

The late Colonel Myddelton Biddulph, of Chirk Castle, who owned this property, told me that on a certain occasion his ancestor and the then Sir Watkin Wynn and Thomas Puleston were dining together, when Thomas Puleston casually mentioned that he would not mind selling his Chirk farms. Nothing more was said; but when the owner of Chirk Castle reached home that night, he sent a groom off to Emral, there and then, to ask for the refusal of the property, so afraid was he of Sir Watkin buying it. This property came to Sir Roger Puleston in right of his wife, Miss Edwards, of Chirk. I have now a vast number of Charters of Chirk and a survey of Chirk lands in the time of Richard II., which is considered a very valuable MS., and which came by this marriage. Thomas Puleston must have given plenty of employment to builders and workmen from 1724 to the end of his life. From 1724 to 1727 he was engaged in building two new wings to Emral : I have the receipt for £1115 in payment of the last instalment. In February, 1726, and in May, 1727, they were paid £160 for rebuilding the front of Emral.

Since that time Emral House has not been altered in any way. As far as I can judge from an old picture that I have before me, previous to these alterations the wings were much shorter than they are now, and the corners of the quadrangle were filled by square buildings. Almost as soon as Thomas Puleston had completed this work he pulled down his stables and built the present ones, which were not completed until 1735. I have the bills for these " new " stables and other work. Richard Trubshaw and Joseph Evans carried out all this work, which was right well done, and has stood the test of time. Thomas Puleston married his cousin, Mary Thelwell, 16th December, 1718, but their married life was a short one, as she died on her way to Bath, 1727. I have a portrait of Thomas Puleston and his wife, also one of Earl Mulgrave, K.G., who in the reign of Queen Elizabeth greatly distinguished himself in the defeat of the Spanish Armada, and which came into our possession through this marriage. Thomas Puleston, like his father, died of fever, and was buried at Worthenbury, 12th June, 1735. Among other legacies, he left £30 to his chaplain and £500 to build a new church at Worthenbury—the present one—which was commenced in 1736 and consecrated 1739. I have a curious letter given me by Lord Hanmer from Thomas Chalinor, dated 16th June, 1735, addressed to—

Thomas Hanmer, Esq., of the Fenns, M.P. for
  Castle Rising,
   at his house, New Bond Street,
    Against Conduit Street.

" I have now got some news to send you, but it is of an ill kind. Mr. Puleston, of Emrall, being dead of a fever, was buried at Worthenbury on Thursday last, where I attended, and believe it to be the mournfullest funeral that ever I saw, he being mightily lamented by persons of all ranks. He was buried after the manner he lived, in great splendour and plenty. There were fixed at the gate twelve porters with black gowns, who, when the corpse removed from the Hall, they with black staves walked before it ; after the hearse went four mourning coaches filled with mourners in cloaks, and likewise twelve men on horseback with cloaks.

There was a very good appearance of gentlemen, and of all other sorts without number. It is computed that his funeral will cost above a £1000.

As I come now to the building of the present church, resulting from Thomas Puleston's legacy, it seems fitting that I should write here all I can find out about the present and previous churches at Worthenbury. Pennant, in his Tour in North Wales, describes Worthenbury Church as "a new neat building dedicated to St. Deiniol, a rectory taken out of Bangor and made a separate Parish by an Act 2 William and Mary, in the presentation of the family of Emral. The name in the Domesday Book is Hurdingberie. Before the Conquest it was held by Earl Edwin. Deiniol was the son of Dunawd. He assisted his father in the establishment of the monastery of Bangor Iscoed. He is said by Geoffry of Monmouth to have died in 544, and was buried at Bardsey.

"The churches founded by him are Llanddeiniol in Cardiganshire, another of the same name in Monmouthshire, Hawarden and Worthenbury in Flintshire, Llanuwchllyn in Merionethshire, and St. Daniel's in Pembrokeshire "

This is Pennant's account, and no doubt it is all that can be gathered, briefly put, of the patron saint and founder of our church. From an earlier date even than 544 there has probably been a church of some sort here, beginning in the 3rd or 4th century with a structure of wattle and daub, which was replaced from time to time as needed, until, as tradition says, a church of brick and timber was built, which was pulled down in 1736, and the present structure placed exactly on the same site. The old church must have been of some size and importance, as the population of the parish at that time was, I believe, greater than it is now. That there must have been a church and burial ground on the present site from a very early period, must be evident to a casual observer who will walk round the present churchyard, as he will see how the soil has been raised by continuous burials for some thirteen centuries.

In the present day there is a feeling that it is desirable to do away with pews. The following account is somewhat amusing of a dispute which took place about a pew in Worthenbury Church about 200 years ago; this, of course, relates to the former church. Pews appear then to have been a coveted possession, and to have been looked upon as marks of importance. The paper will explain itself : " Edward Griffiths, an inhabitant of Worthenbury Parish, his account of what he hath heard his father and other 'antient' people of the said Parish relate concerning the seats in the said church. The Church of Worthenbury was formerly a chapelrie belonging to the parish of Bangor, till of late years Sir Roger Puleston caused it to be made into a parish Church at his own proper charge ; and about eighty years ago it had no settled forms or seats in it, save only the two chief houses in the parish, viz., Emral and Broughton, had ' pues ' in it, and settled forms for themselves and their families. The family of Emral had two seats near the pulpit, the lower of which was given by Sir Roger Puleston, predecessor to Judge Puleston in Emral Estate, to his chief servant, one Burton, who held a good tenement under his master, where his wife and family sate during her life. After Mrs. Burton's death the seat was given to Mr. Holliman by Judge Puleston for his wife (who was a near kinswoman to the Judge's wife) and his familie to sit in, who always sate in it since that time without any molestation or hindrance, or any claim of any other person that have any pretence or hold, have.

" The body of the church had only moveable seats or benches to sitt on as their abilitie or con-venience would allow, till about eighty years ago, a well disposed man, being rich and having no children, was at the charge of making settled forms in the body of the said church, which he left in common to the inhabitants of the said parish to sit in, having no power to appropriate any of them to any particular inhabitant. I have seen, and I think as yet may be seen in an old register of our Parish of Worthenberie, an order made in the Bishop's Court in Chester about the time the said church was unfurnished with seats, wherein is declared that no claim shall be made in the body of the church to any particular seat, which order was caused thus. A sub-stantial inhabitant of the said parish, who held a good tenement in the said parish upon lease, did erect a seat for himself and familie to sit in the body of the church, at which the other inhabitants did complain, being grieved at his presumption to be above them. They had a citation for his appear-

II

ance at the court in Chester, and then this order was made in the said court, and he was compelled to disclaim and disown any title to the said seate or any other seate in the said church, to which order he did then subscribe."

This seems to show that the said church was not a very small one, or one of indifferent structure, as William Griffiths seems to take us to the beginning of the 17th century, some 250 years before the present church was built. My belief is that the old church was much the same in size as the present one, without the present chancel, the old chancel ending where the present one begins. The following correspondence seems to bear out this assumption. It was between Thomas Puleston, of Emral, and John Whitehall, of Broughton, dated, Emrall, 9-29-1721.

"Dear Sir,—We are very much concerned to hear of your indisposition, and heartily wish you a speedy recovery. The reason of my giving you this trouble will, I hope, plead my excuse. I am going to make some alteration in the Chancel and Church at Worthenbury, and, by all that I can learn or imagine, the chancel entirely belongs to me. There has been part of it in which your lady sits taken out of that seat in which Holliman and Hugh Puleston sits, which, as I was informed, was done during a minority. I would therefore desire to be informed from yourself how this matter stands. The Chancel must undoubtedly belong to me only, in whose family the tithes were, and if I go on with my design of building I must believe you will resign that (seat) and I hope the accommodating this matter in your lifetime may be so far from making the least breach of friendship between us now, that it may be the means of preventing any disturbance hereafter of that harmony which I desire may always subsist between your family and that of, Sir,

Your affectionate friend and servant,

"THOS. PULESTON."

COPY OF MEMORANDUM OF ANSWER WRITTEN ON THE BACK OF THE LETTER.

"Happening to be at Chester at the time Mr. Jones delivered your letter, I received my father's command to thank you for your kind expressions of concern for his illness. I thank God he's better than what he has been, but he says a matter of such conse-quence concerning which you write deserves more serious consideration than what at present he's able

to allow it, before a definite answer be given, and,
indeed, so great yet is his disorder that he finds in
himself a disposition of consulting not anything so
much as his own ease and quiet. But this he
desires that I'll remind you of, that the family of
Broughton have immemorially buried on that side
the Chancel where the servants sit, and he daresay
you will be of an opinion that it is no inconsider-
able thing to give up such a right. It would be my
father's greatest pleasure to have it in his power to
oblige Mr. Puleston, and that there be perpetual
harmony betwixt the two families is very much his
desire, yet not more than it is the ambition of, Sir,

" Yours, etc."

NOTE ALSO WRITTEN AT THE BACK OF THE LETTER.

" My father confesses that some part of the pew
wherein my mother sits was taken out of that in
which T. Holyman and H. Puleston are seated in
. church, and the reason was this, the foresaid seat to
which you now lay claim, did equally belong to the
two families of Emral and Broughton, and used to
be the sitting place of the younger brothers of both
houses. But from the time the seat you mention of
my father's was enlarged you've had that seat entirely

to yourself, and all rights and title on our part have been disclaimed. This, my father says, is the true state of the case as far forth as his memory is capable of carrying him."

I am very much indebted to my kinsman, Mr. P. Davies Cooke, for sending me these letters, as they mark very plainly where the chancel of the church of 1735 ended. As we know exactly where the Broughton's family vault is, and as this was near their pew, there seems little doubt that in 1721 the Broughton pew was very much where it is now and the Emral pew on the opposite side, and probably, when the present church was built, a new vault was made for the Emral family under the present chancel, including in it the vault in which Judge Puleston, his wife, and other members of the family, and Thomas Puleston, by whose posthumous work the present church was built, were buried.

Thomas Puleston, as we have seen, had for some years an intention of making alterations and improvements in the Chancel of Worthenbury, but he was apparently delayed by the illness of Mr. John Whitehall; but now he seems to have the Parish with him in this work; and I find that the churchwardens were collecting money towards the building fund, as the following receipt will show.

"I do hereby acknowledge to have received this day from Daniel Pritchard and of the Churchwardens of the Parish of Worthenbury, in the County of Flint, the sum of £168, being part of the money collected by a brief towards re-building the Parish Church of Worthenbury aforesaid, which said sum I promise to be accountable for on demand to the Parish. Witness my hand.

"Thos. Puleston.

"21st September, 1732.

"Witness, R. Jones, Rector.

"Ellis Wynn."

"March 22nd, 1736.

"Received of Madam Puleston, executrix of Thomas Puleston, Esq., late of Emrall, deceased, the above sum of £168, being part of the money collected by briefs towards the re-building of the Parish Church of Worthenbury, which sum I received of the brief gatherers and deposited in the hands of the said Thomas Puleston for safe custody, I say, received the said sum by the hands of Mr. Kirk.   "Daniel Pritchard."

In 1736 Thomas Lloyd, of Overton, Esq., John
Puleston, of Pickhill, Esq. and the Rector, acting
trustees, agreed with Mr. John Kirk, Emral agent,
to build a new church for £955, towards which they
had collected £170 10s. 6d., and £500 left by the
will of Thomas Puleston, of Emrall, Esq., which
sums, together with £30 allowed for the old church,
amount in the whole to £700 10s. 6d. The remainder
is to be paid by the benevolence of the neighbouring
gentry and a lea (rate) on the parish.

"They began to pull down the old church May
11th, and the Rector and congregation went to Emrall
Chapel 16th. The old chancel was removed to a
corner of the churchyard to put the font in to
baptize children." This seems to make it clear that
this old church was built of brick and timber, or
they could not have removed the chancel to a
corner of the churchyard. The price the contractor allowed for the old materials proves that
this church must have been of considerable size.
There are no remains that I know of it, except
an old oak chest in the belfry, two very curious old
oak collecting boxes with " rember the poor " carved
on them, and possibly the double doors of the vestry :

but it is almost certain that some of the oak used in the construction of the roof had been in the old Church.

We find by an entry in our registers that in 1737, April 26th, a marriage was solemnised between John Reed, of Holt, and Margaret Gregory, of this parish, spinster, which took place in the old chancel by virtue of a licence granted by the Chancellor. A few weeks later there is this entry in the register: " William Jones, of Eastyn and Catherine Edwards, laundry maid at Emrall, in this parish, banns being first published three times in both parishes, and certified by the Vicar of Eastyn, were, with the Rector's leave, married by Mr. Docksey in Emrall Chapel, 16th May, 1737." There is another entry in the following year of great interest to me: " Anne, daughter of John Puleston, of Emrall, and Anne, his wife, was born 23rd March, 1738. She immediately received private baptism from Mr. Docksey, the chaplain, and public baptism at Emrall Chapel from the Rector, April 21st." This baptism seems almost in my time, as she died in my lifetime, and was the mother of my grandfather, the first baronet of Emral, and wife of Richard Parry

Price, of Brynypys. Her son was well known in this parish and neighbourhood as a kindly neighbour, a good landlord, and a master of foxhounds. There are still some few at this time alive (1895), who knew and respected him.

The building of the church went steadily on, and it was consecrated in 1739. Unfortunately, I have no authenticated picture of the old church in which Philip Henry preached. I have a picture of an old black and white church with a small belfry, such as I suppose Worthenbury old church had been, but I am not sure it represents this church; neither is there any picture, that I know of, of the old chapel at Emral, where the wedding and baptism I have just told of took place. It had a cure of souls attached to it, and a burial ground. The last person, tradition says, that was buried there was a black man, (probably a black servant, as there was a great "fashion" for black footmen in the last century). The only remains that I can discover of this chapel are an old door studded with nails, which at this time is the house door at John Prince's, at Wallington, the two shields of stone of the Puleston arms and quarterings, which are now let into the garden wall at Emral, which were said to have been on the pillars of the entrance to the chapel; some of the stained glass now in the east window of Worthenbury Church, and some of the prayer books in my pew in the chancel. This chapel stood in front of Emrall House near the corner of the garden wall. I have spoken to persons who professed to have seen it. There is little doubt that the locality of it is tolerably accurate; to mark the site two or three trees have been planted there. It is a very singular thing that trees planted on the spot always refused to grow, so I planted the ones now there, a few yards right and left.

It was John Puleston, who was buried at Worthenbury, 9th June, 1775, who pulled this chapel down, where so many of his people had been baptized, and certainly a namesake of his buried 300 years before. He is said to have been thrown from his horse on the spot where the chapel stood, and to have died of the injuries he then received. The date of this pulling down was about 1775, and this would be something like sixty-five years before the time old William Almond spoke to me of it, yet he seemed to recollect it perfectly. Strange to say, I find an ominous silence in the Emral MSS. as to the pulling down of this chapel.

The parish registers are in very good condition, and date from 1597, from which time also there is a list of ministers and churchwardens. For the first few years each page seems to have been written at one time, as if from a note book. The names of two churchwardens and John Meredith, curate, are at the bottom of each page. The cover and leaves of our old register book are of vellum, and at first the entries are very simple, and little of interest is recorded. In 1608 Mr. Edwards is in charge, and his writing is most difficult to read. In 1620 there are no signatures of either minister or churchwardens. There is a memorandum that on the 4th November, 1631, thirty-four shillings and sixpence halfpenny was collected for the poor of Wrexham at a "general fast at Worthenbury for the removal of the plague that then raged. Thos. Pritchard, curate."

This seems to have been a very liberal and creditable subscription, seeing that the value of money was then very different from what it is now. Mr. Pritchard wrote the entries in Latin, and it is with great difficulty I can make them out. The marriage of Johannes Puleston and Elizabetha Wolrich is fairly legible, and is recorded as having taken place in December, 1635. Mr. Smith succeeded Mr. Pritchard, but he did not trouble the registers much, as in 1642 there is no entry at all, and only one in 1643, and in 1644 there is an entry of the burial of Thomas, son of John Adams, curate of Worthenbury, and this is the only one made. 1645, no entry. In 1646 three baptisms are recorded, one of them being the son of the curate. At the end of the year, across the register, is written the following couplet,

Learn the Lord and then thou wilt see,
That happy for ever then thou wilt be.

In 1647, there is an entry of a marriage only. 1648, no entry. 1649, two entries, one of them being added seven years afterwards. 1650, Rowland Broughton and Elizabeth Broughton were married, 2nd June; there are also two burials. 1651, there are four entries. 1652, the number is considerably increased. 1653-4, one entry only in each year. After 1655 things seem more settled, and a more satisfactory state is observed in our registers.

Generally throughout England during the troubles of Charles I. with his Parliament, as well as during Cromwell's time, church matters of all kinds fell into a neglected state. At this time, however, Worthenbury was highly favoured, for Philip Henry came to the parish, and the first entry in his distinct and precise handwriting is as follows : " John Broughton, of Broughton, was burryed, September 4th, 1655." In 1656, " Richard, the son of John Puleston, was buryed." " Thomas Broughton, of Broughton, Gent, was buryed 4th October, 1658," and 7th October, "Elizabeth, wife of Judge Puleston, was burryed ;" and in the following year, 1659, "the Honble. John Puleston, of Emerall, Justice of the Court of Common Pleas, was burryed 8th day of September." Death had indeed made inroads in these four years in the houses of Broughton and Emral, and sad indeed must have been the time for the inhabitants of our parish.

In 1661 there is the interesting entry " John, the son of Philip Henry, preacher of God's Word in this parish, was baptised, 12th May." In Mr. Henry's business book we find, " John Henry, born at Worthenbury, Friday, 3rd May, 1661," and on the same page the touching notice, " John Henry, our firstborn, and the son of our hopes, departed this life at Whitchurch, Friday, April 12th, about sun sett, and lyes burryed towards the upper part of the middle ' Isle ' in the church there, 1667." So that during the few years with which Philip Henry had been connected with Worthenbury, death, who knocks equally at all our doors, had three times visited Emral and twice Broughton, and did not even spare this holy good man. When Philip Henry was ejected from Worthenbury in 1661, Mr. Hilton succeeded him, but in 1662 Mr. Hilton signs himself Vicar of Hanmer, and Mr. D. Humphreys comes to Worthenbury. In 1665 there is a singular entry in our registers, " Joseph of the Coat, a poor boy libering in this parish, was buryed." In 1669 there is this entry, " Collected, 26th September, for the poor people of Malpas that had lost by fire the sum of [amount destroyed'.

After Worthenbury was separated from Bangor in 1683, Mr. Shore being rector and Mr. Williams curate, there is no superfluous information given about any event that did take place, though he makes one entry which did not take place in the parish—the marriage of Sir Roger Puleston and Mrs. Catherine Edwards—this, however, was by no means an unusual thing. Mr. Shore makes up for a good deal of his brevity in his entries in the registers by the clearness of his handwriting, which proves that he was generally speaking a man of few words : there are, however, exceptions to this when he enters the burial of Mrs. Audrey Broughton in 1695, April 24th, " being sixty-nine years of age and wife to John Broughton, of Broughton, Esq., forty-three years." He enters, " Sir Roger Puleston, of Emerall, died in London, February 28th, 1697, and was buried at Gresford, 4th March." Old maids were evidently a rarity in Mr. Shore's day, as he records in 1711 the burial of Jane Wynne, " an ancient maid of Sutton Green in the County of Denby," " Mrs. Hanna Shore, wife of Mr. John Shore, Rector of this parish, youngest daughter of Thomas Clyve, Esq., of Walford, in the county of Salop. She died, January 1st and was buried Saturday, 5th January, 1712." This is a remarkable instance of name and lineage being fully recorded in a parish register. After Mr. Shore lost his wife, his handwriting shows that his health began to fail, and on January 14th, 1714, there is an entry, "Joshua Powel and Elizabeth Palin, both of this parish, were married" by Mr. Appleton, Curate, by licence. This is the first instance recorded in this parish of a marriage by license.

On 26th January, 1714, "Mr. John Shore, Rector of Worthenbury, was buried." On the 8th July, in the same year, his successor was buried in Northamptonshire. His name was Mr. John Gent, who was followed by Mr. Owen Lloyd, who died at Pengwern, May 17th, 1718. The poor man seems to have been ill the whole of the time he was rector of Worthenbury, which may account for there being no entry in our registers from October, 1715, to July, 1718. A note in them tells that "Robert Jones, clerk, was presented to the said rectory by Thomas Puleston, of Emrall, Esq., on Monday, 19th May, instituted by Doctor Wainwright, Chancellor of the Diocesse, on Tuesday, June 17th, and inducted by Andrew Lloyd, Curate of Overton, on Friday, 20th June, 1718." In 1744, Robert Jones died after an incumbency of twenty-six years. There is a curious entry in the register by this rector dated July 19th, 1719, "Whereas, Dorothy, the wife of Robert Jones, clerk, rector, doth sit in the Parish Church of

Worthenbury, in the seat of William Lloyd, of
Halghton, Esq., I do hereby acknowledge that she
sits in the said seat by the special leave and permission of the said William Lloyd, Esq., and not by
any claim or right that I, as Rector of Worthenbury,
can have to the same. R. Jones, Rector of
Worthenbury." This lady did not live long to
enjoy Mr. Lloyd's kindness, as she died in Shrewsbury, 25th December, 1720.

Unfortunately, as we approach nearer our own
time, instead of the registers being carefully and
accurately kept, they seem to be more and more
irregular, and to have been left to the tender mercy
of the parish clerk. There is no notice of the
appointment of a successor to Mr. Jones, and
between 1749 and 1755 there is an absence of entries
in the registers for which I can give no account. In
the latter year new register books are established,
one for marriages with printed forms to fill in, and a
blank book for burials and christenings. This com-
mences with a notification that the " Rev. Richard
Jones, M.A., resigned the living of Worthenbury,
May 26th, 1755, when Philip Puleston, clerk, M.A.,
was presented to the said rectory by Robert Williams

and Robert Davies, Esqs., instituted by Samuel Peploe, B.L., Chancellor of the Diocese, August 15th, and inducted by the Rev. William Phillips, Rector of Bangor, August 25th, 1755. N.B.—Robert Williams and Robert Davies, Esquires, presented for this turn only." The only mention of the previous rector, Mr. Richard Jones, is the one mentioned above, Mr. Ravencroft signing himself curate. So it is not certain that Mr. Richard Jones succeeded Mr. Robert Jones. The Rev. Philip Puleston, afterwards Doctor of Divinity, resided a good deal at Pickhill Hall; he was the fourth son of John Puleston, of Pickhill; but eventually succeeded to the property. He would easily get over to Worthenbury from there, and until 1787, at almost all the marriages solemnised at Worthenbury, he was the officiating minister. Then he became vicar also of Ruabon and may have resided there. He was married to his first wife in Worthenbury Church; she, however, had not far to come, as she was Mary Egerton, of Broxton, in the parish of Malpas. This was in 1766, she died 1772. He died in 1801. The old book of "offices" which is now in use, was a gift from him, and for more than one hundred years the baptismal and burial services have been read from it.

In the year 1788 a marriage is entered in our registers between Simon Parry and Elizabeth Hallmark, " by licence." Two months later these people are re-married after banns. A daughter of theirs, Mrs. Hollins, was living in Worthenbury in 1872, and gave the following explanation of this: The bride was under age, and old Mr. Peter Whitehall Davies, of Broughton, had a particular objection to marriages by licence, and as he had always taken a great interest in the Hallmarks, persuaded them to be married over again. From this marriage sprang my two old friends, James and John Parry, of whom I have already written.

To show what a loyal place Worthenbury was, and I trust always will be, I have copied the following from our registers :—

" The insertion of the following names in this register is intended to be a lasting monument of the zeal and loyalty of the inhabitants of this parish in coming forward in defence of their king and their country, their religion, liberty and laws at this important and critical juncture, when a

sanguinary and inveterate foe, by a long projected
invasion, threatens them all with immediate
destruction.   March 3rd, 1798.

£

		£		
" Lieut.-Colonel Puleston, Ancient British Fencibles, per annum during the war	... ...	100		
" Mrs. Puleston	... ...	50		
" Peter Whitehall Davies, Esq. ...		50		
" Mrs. Whitehall Davies		50		
" Rev. Wh. Wh. Davies	...	15		
" Rev. Dr. Puleston ...	...	20		
" Worthenbury Society	...	10		
" Other Items, making...	...	£329	4	6 "

Mr. Ethelston, who succeeded Dr. Puleston as rector
of Worthenbury, did not reside here, and his name
only appears a few times in the registers, though he
was rector for more than thirty years.   He was, I
believe, a Canon of the Collegiate Church of Man-
chester, now the cathedral; so from 1787, when Dr.
Puleston ceased, as far as is known, to officiate in
the church, until 1831, when the Rev. Hugh Mathie
was inducted, the rector's name scarcely appears in
the registers.

Soon after Mr. Mathie became rector, he pulled down the old rectory which Judge Puleston had built for Philip Henry, and re-built it at his own expense, at a cost of about £1700 ; I believe it was finished in 1833. He had, however, the good taste to preserve Philip Henry's study just as it was when he occupied it, the flooring boards, beams, and the shape being in much the same state as they were some 200 years ago. The Rectory House is un-altered since Mr. Mathie's day, though I have added a bed-room and a dressing-room on the south side, with a pantry, work-room, and small hall for servants beneath it. I have also built a cow-house for three cows, pig-stye, loose box, brew-house, and bake-house at a cost of about £400, which I am glad to say has not been charged on the living. The church, which was built mainly with Thomas Puleston's money, is identically as it was first built.

Mr. Mathie was a very good rector and an ex-cellent preacher; he was, however, rather addicted to thumping the cushion, and on one occasion he knocked over one of the brass candle-holders, on which he said, in a very audible aside, " There goes

the candlestick," and then quietly went on with his
discourse. As long as he was in health he was
much liked in the parish for his kindness and attention to the poor. Mr. Mathie died in 1843, and was
succeeded by the Rev. Charles Wynne Eyton, who
was a Fellow of Jesus College, Oxford. He was
appointed to a college living in 1848 (Aston Clinton,
Bucks), and then I came here.

I think it may be of interest to give here an
estimate I have found among the Emral papers
for building Worthenbury Church, which I believe
was acted on, and the specifications carried out,
with some additions, which apparently cost about
an extra £100 : "An estimate of all charges, find-
ing all materials, as stone, brick, timber, boards,
iron, glass, lead, slates, laths, nails, carriage, and
workmanship, and finish everything given me according to the design of Mr. Trubshaw. The particulars
are as follows : To sink down four feet six inches
deep and bring up a substantial foundation round
the church three feet six inches thick, and round
the tower five feet thick, and to be of brick and
stone up to the level of the surface, and from the
said surface to build the church forty-six feet long,

thirty-two feet broad, and eighteen feet high to the cornice ; the walls to be two feet six inches thick, the plinth on the outside to be two feet high, to be of stone, and stone round the windows, as in the design, each window to be five feet wide and twelve feet high—find good glass and strong iron for the same. The cornice to be of stone, and stone rails, and the parapet wall to be of brick, as in the design. The tower to be twenty feet square at the bottom, and fifty-eight feet high to the top of the wall, and ornaments above, as in the design, the walls to be three feet six inches thick, from thence up to the second floor three feet thick, from thence to the top cornice two feet six inches, the parapet wall to be one brick and a half thick, and coped with stone, and all the ornaments as in the design : the top of the tower to be leaded with good lead, about eight and a half lbs. to the foot. Find boards for doors and for four floors in the tower, and a round staircase up to the second floor, and two ladders to the top of tower. Find good glass for four round windows, and good iron and boards for the four windows at the top as designed. The body of the church to be eighteen feet high from the floor to the ceiling; the iles to be laid with stone, and the bottom of all the pews to be boarded, the seats or pewing to be designed as in the design, and to be wainscotted four feet three inches high, the outsides to be quarter round work and out of good dry oak boards; and make a handsome plain pulpit and sound board, and find good iron hinges and bolts for all the pew doors, and purge all the inside of the church with good lime and hair mortar. The roof of the church to be pitch pine, and slated with good blue slates, and a lead gutter round the body of the church, the narrowest place to be eighteen inches broad, and every foot of lead to weigh eight and a half lbs. to the foot, and find good sound timber for all the roof, and to finish all the before mentioned work in a substantion manner for £735. To build the alcove or chancel according to the plan, and upright the walls to be in height with the body of the church and thickness. The three windows the same, with good glass and substantial ironwork, done in the best manner, and find good lead for the gutter, and slates and timber for the roof, and purge the inside

of it with good lime and hair, and pave the floor
with stone.   All will come   £75
                              £735
                              ─────

The whole total   £810
                  ─────

" Trubshaw's proposal for building Worthenbury
Church, £810."

After 155 years' wear and tear, I think the judgment of all who know anything of building must be
that the contractor did his work honestly and well ;
the original slates are still on the roof, a great deal
of the same glass in the windows, and everything
remains much as it was, except a new beam that
Mr. Dodd of Whitchurch put in the chancel ceiling
for me, in place of one that was literally dust and
ashes, and that I re-slated the chancel.   The north
side of the church roof had to be repaired some
years ago, however, the result of a fire, when the
church had a narrow escape of being burned down ;
this took place one Sunday evening about eight
o'clock, when I was summoned with the unpleasant
intelligence that the church was on fire ; and on fire
it was, with a raging wind and sparks flying as high

as the tower. I sent for my carpenter, Thomas Roberts, and told him to take his axe and saw, and use them freely, at the same time ordering the church flue to be plugged with sacks at the bottom. Roberts most pluckily carried out his directions, and thus saved the church. Roberts was the contractor to build our school-room, and did the work remarkably well.

I have heaps of household bills of the date when our church was built, and these plainly show how the church was built for so small a sum of money : a labourer's wages were then 4d. a day, and, of course, skilled labour in proportion ; beef and mutton being about 2d. per lb.

The bells in our tower were, as we have seen, not included in the contract ; they were cast at Gloucester, and were hung in 1746.

1st bell.—Peace, good neighbourhood. 1746.

2nd bell.—Prosperity to the Parish. A. G. R.

3rd bell.—We were all cast at Gloucester by E. & B. Rudhall. 1746.

4th bell.—Daniel Woolams and John Lewis, Churchwardens. A. G. R. 1746.

In the body of the church there is a very handsome brass chandelier, which was given in the year

1816, by Mr. William Lea, of Halghton. The communion table is adorned by an altar cloth, with embroidered curtains and kneeling cushion, given and worked by my wife (Lady Puleston). The communion plate is very plain and handsome, and is all of Queen Anne date; there is a very fine flagon given by some unknown friend in memory of Captain Robert Holliman, with the date 1703 engraved on it. The chalice and paten are somewhat worn. There is a good plain round silver plate on which the bread is placed before it is consecrated. All this plate bears the " Britannia " mark. The two handsome carved oak chairs inside the communion rails were given at long intervals: one by Sir Richard Puleston, second Baronet of Emral, the second by Mr. Howard, of Broughton, on the occasion of his sister's marriage in Worthenbury Church.

There are four charities belonging to the Parish of Worthenbury. All the moneys belonging to these charities is in the hands of the Charity Commissioners of England, the interest being quarterly paid to me as rector. The most important of these charities is a sum of £666, left by Emma Elizabeth, widow of Sir Richard Puleston, first Baronet of

Emral, the income of which is £18 6s. 8d., to be
given in soup and clothing to the poor. There is
also a bread charity left by Mr. Jones, who was an
architect in Chester, and who was connected with
Worthenbury Parish, of the annual value of £5 10s.,
which is to be given in the Parish Church to those
deserving poor persons who attend the service there.
Another Mr. Jones left a sum of £100 I believe,
to be given in clothing ; the value of this is
£3 0s. 4d. per annum.   The fourth is a sum of £50
less legacy duty, which was left by my old friend
and neighbour, Maria Howell, the value of which is
about 20s. per annum, but nothing has been received
on account of this charity, as it had only been in
the hands of the Charity Commissioners a few
months, when her brother, James Howell, died.
The interest is to be given in any way the rector
may determine.

Our churchyard has been added to, I think, when
Mr. Matthie was rector, but it sorely needs now to
be increased in size.   The yew trees now growing
there, seedlings from the rectory garden, were
planted by me about 1860.

I think, with the occupation of the House of

Emral at the death of John Puleston, of whom I
have already written, I have about completed the
task I set myself. He left Emral to his nephew
Richard, curiously passing over his sister Anne,
who married Richard Parry Price, of Brynypys,
23rd October, 1764, at a place called Biddulph, in
Staffordshire, by the Rev. John Gresley. In Mr.
Parry Price's diary, which is in my possession, this
event is thus recorded : "Made the happiest man in
the world by being married to my dearest Nancy at
Biddulph." Curious to tell, the diary ends there!
Mrs. Parry Price seems to have managed the Emral
property for her son during his minority, though I
believe she lived at Brynypys till the death at all
events of her husband, who died 14th May, 1782, at
the early age of forty-five. He, as well as his widow,
was buried in the old Priory at Birkenhead, almost
all of which parish belonged to him, as well as the
Birkenhead Ferry and the land on which the present
docks stand. He was a relative of the Right Rev.
Richard Parry, Bishop of St. Asaph. Mr. John
Puleston and Mr. Edward Puleston were present
at the Bishop's funeral, September, 1623.

Richard Puleston was born in 1765, and succeeded to the property in 1775. His godfathers at his baptism were Sir Nigel Gresley and Thomas Puleston, of Emral. He was High Sheriff for Flintshire in 1793. In 1813 he was created a baronet by George III. As Colonel of the Ancient British Fencibles, a regiment raised by Sir Watkin Wynn, he saw some service during the Irish Rebellion, and was present at the battles of Arklow and Vinegar Hill and Carnew, at the last of which his horse was shot from under him, and his life was saved by Tom Crane, a Worthenbury man, galloping up to him with a led horse. Sir Richard was a personal friend of the Prince Regent, the Prince of Wales, whom he introduced into his Principality, and I bear an oak tree as a crest, with a shield with the Prince of Wales' plume hanging on it, granted in commemoration of the event.

Sir Richard was himself honoured by a visit from the Duke of Clarence at Emral, and the Royal Duke mentions, in a letter to his host, how pleased he was with a horse Sir Richard had mounted him on when at Emral. Sir Richard's widow left the letters of the Royal family at her death to Mr. Wynne of Peniarth, who, through his mother, was descended

from the Pulestons of Pickhill, to which property
his father succeeded on the death of Doctor
Puleston. Sir Richard was succeeded in May,
1840, in the Emral property by his only son, who
was colonel of the Royal Flintshire Regiment of
Rifles. He also served the office of High Sheriff for
Flintshire, I think, in 1844 or 1845. When he died in
1860, he was succeeded by his eldest son, Richard
Price Puleston, who died August, 1893.

The last people who lived at Emral, which they
left in 1861, were Mr. and Mrs. Peel Ethelston, who
rented it from the second baronet, who never cared
to live there after the death of his wife ; when they
left Emral for Hinton, the old house was dismantled
and has been in a state of neglect ever since. Mr.
Ethelston is a grandson of the Mr. Ethelston who
was Rector of Worthenbury for some years.

The principal monuments in the church are those
to Rev. Dr. Puleston, Broughton Whitehall ;
W. Whitehall Davies, of Broughton and Llanerch ;
George Allanson, Prebend of Ripon and Rector of
Hodnet ; Sir Richard Puleston, 1st Baronet ; Sir
Richard Price Puleston, 3rd Baronet ; Hugh
Matthie, Rector. A tablet to Watkin Hayman,

a monument to Mary Louisa Bailey, and another to her mother, Elizabeth Puleston; and two brasses, one to the memory of Sir Richard Puleston, 2nd Baronet, and his children, and another to Annabella Anne Thoyts, one of his daughters.

In order to bring down the history of the parish to the present time, April, 1895, I must mention the names of the first Parish Council: The Rector, chairman; Mr. William Houlbrooke, vice-chairman: Mr. John Astbury, Mr. John William Jones, Mr. D. E. Chalton, Mr. Reuben Prince, and Mr. John Woodfield, with Mr. William Robert Urmson, clerk; he is also parish organist and schoolmaster, an office he has filled with very great credit and ability for eighteen years: and he is ably assisted in his important duties by his wife, and Miss Susan Poynton as sewing mistress. The Rev. Tom Watson is our present curate, vice F. B. Roberts, promoted to be Vicar of Bettisfield. Mr. Edward Rogers is parish clerk and sexton.

My task is now completed—I own imperfectly—but such as it is I with some hesitation put it before those who have an interest in the neighbourhood and parish.

A LIST OF THE MINISTERS AND CHURCHWARDENS OF WORTHENBURY FROM 1597.

Ministers.		*Churchwardens.*
1597	John Meredith, Curate.	William Jenkins ; David Richards.
1598	Do.	William ; Thomas Griffiths.
1599	Do.	Thomas Randle ; John Swirdall.
1600	Do.	Do.
1601	Do.	David Thomas ; Edward ap Griffith.
1602	Do.	Do.
1603	Do.	John William Jenkin; Richard Puleston.
1604	Do.	Do.
1605	Do.	John Downward ; William.
1606	Do.	Do.
1607	Do.	John Partington ; Richard Morgan.
1608	John Edwards, Curate.	Roger Maunsell ; Richard Lanneson.
1609	Do.	Do.
1610	John Roberts, Curate.	Do.
1611	Do.	John Morgan.
1612	Do.	David Roger ; Humphrey.
1613	Do.	Thomas Griffiths ; Randle Lewis.
1614	Do.	Edward Phelips ; John Davies.
1615	Do.	Do.
1616	Do.	John Downward.
1617	Do.	John Tindale ; John James.
1618	Do.	— Maunsell ; John Wynne.

13

	Ministers.	*Churchwardens.*
1619	John Roberts, Curate.	Griff Rowland.
1620	Do.	No signatures.
1621	Do.	John Roberts ; Morgan ap John.
1622	Do.	Richard Puleston ; Humphrey Gothia.
1623	Thomas Pritchard.Curate.	Edward Williams ; Thomas Davies.
1624	Do.	Roger — ; Morgan —.
1625	Do.	— Puleston.
1626	Do.	— Downward ; — ap Willan.
1627	Do.	
1628	Do.	John ; John James.
1629	Do.	Ralph Maunsell ; John Barn
1630	Do.	
1631	Do.	John Rogers ; Thomas John Wynne.
1632	Do.	Richard Puleston
1633	Do.	
1634	Do.	
1635	Do.	
1636	Do.	John ap Morgan ; Richardus. (?)
1637		
1638		
1639		
1640		
1641	Smyth, Curate.	Mr. Roger Puleston ; Thomas Phillips.
1642		
1643		
1644	John Adams, Curate.	
1645	Do.	
1646	Do.	
1647	No entries ; troublous times.	
1648	Do.	
1649	Do.	
1650	Do.	
1651	Do	

Ministers.	*Churchwardens.*

1652 No entries ; troublous times.

1653   Do.

1654   Do.

1655 Philip Henry, Minister.

1656   Do.

1657   Do.   John Holliman : Roger Puleston.

1658   Do.   Do.

1659   Do.   Do.

1660   Do.   Leonard Perkins ; Edward Davies.

1661 Richard Hilton, Curate.   Do.

1662   Do.   Minister. Matthews.

1662 D. Humphreys, Curate.   Griffith ap John ; Tresham Matthews.

1663   Do.   John Hughes ; Edward Mondith.

1664   Do.   Edward Rogers ; John Andrews.

1665   Do.   Edward Weaver ; Richard Eyton.

1666   Do.   Thomas Pugh ; Daniel Pritchard.

1667   Do.   Roger Downward ; George Morgan.

1668 D. Humphreys.

1668-9 Thomas Walmer.

1669 William Whittle.

1670   Do.

1671 William Whittle, Minister. John Birch ; John Griffith.

1672   Do.

1673   Do.

1674   Do.

1675   Do.   John Robert.

1676

1677 D. Lyon Capell

1678   Do.   Griffiths, for — tenement John Evan ·

1679   Do.   John — ; John —.

1680 Nat. Williams, Curate.   George Sedgwick ; John Griffiths, Jun.

1681   Do.   Mr. John Puleston ; John Andrews.

1682   Do.   Thomas Pritchard ; George Morgan

Ministers.	*Churchwardens.*
1683 John Shore, Rector ; Nat. Williams, Curate until 1691.	Edward ap Hugh ; John Downward.
1684 Do.	Richard Thomas ; T. Drury, Jun.
1685 Do.	Thomas Dale ; Thomas Wynn.
1686 Do.	Roger Jenkin ; John Clutton.
1687 Do.	William Bostock ; John Philips.
1688 Do.	Randle Morgan ; Thomas Matthews.
1689 Do.	Thomas Drury, Sen. ; Edward Hopley.
1690 Do.	Edward Pritchard ; John Maddox,Sarn.
1691 Do.	Randle Moyle ; William Maunsell.
1692 Do.	Thomas Drury ; Francis Clerk.
1693 Do.	John Humphreys ; John Evans, Adravelin.
1694 Do.	John Philips ; John Humphreys.
1695 Do.	Roger Griffith-Wallington ; George Göch.
1696 Do.	Thomas Shone ; Roger Thomas.
1697 Do.	Francis Andrews ; Ed. Spakeman.
1698 Do.	George Morgan, Jun. ; Edward Prichard, Jun.
1699 Do.	J. Evans ; William Bedward for Widow Clerk.
1700 Do.	Ed. Griffiths ; Tristram Matthews.
1701 Do.	George Morgan ; Thomas Brown.
1702 Do.	John Sedgwick ; Thos. Davies.
1703 Do.	Thomas Jenkins ; Thomas Evans.
1704 Do.	Mr. Hugh Puleston ; Thos. Slater.
1705 Do.	Daniel Prichard,Sen. ; Richd. Hanmer.
1706 Do.	Thomas Clerk ; Thos. Griffith, Wern.
1707 Do.	Ed. Hughes ; John Downward.
1708 Do.	Thos. Prichard, Jun. ; John Randle.
1709 Do.	Richard Clerk ; Richard Thomas.

Ministers.	Churchwardens.
1710 John Shore, Rector.	Francis Clerk ; William Club.
1711 Do.	Thomas Prichard ; William Clutton.
1712 Do.	John Griffiths, Adrevelin ; John Peters.
1713 Mr. Appleton, Curate.	John Hanmer ; John Williams.
1714 John Shore died. Joseph Gent, Rector.	Ed. Spakeman, for Widow Sedgwick ; John Blethia.
1715 Owen Lloyd, Rector.	Thos. Griffiths-Wallington ; William Clutton for William Gregory.
1716 Do.	Thomas Shone ; John Rodenhurst.
1717 Do.	Mr. Hugh Puleston ; Richard Powell.
1718 Robert Jones, Rector.	Thomas Drury ; Roger Hanson.
1719 Do.	Randle Moyle : Thos. Andrews.
1720 Piers Lloyd, Curate.	Thomas Ewards ; John Humphreys.
1721 Do.	Thomas Jones ; Robert Caldecot.
1722 Do.	John Newens ; Oliver Moins.
1723 Do.	Roger Brown ; Richard Powell for Thos. Andrews, Quaker.
1724 Robert Jones, Rector.	Thomas Pemberton ; Wm. Shone for his father.
1725 Do.	Joseph Hanson ; John Griffiths, Adrevelin.
1726 Do.	Andrew Cleaton ; Andrew Loyd in Mr. Puleston of Pickhill tenement
1727 Do.	John Kerrison ; Samuel Morris.
1728 Do.	Edward Powel ; Thos. Hughes for Sedgwick's tenement.
1729 Do.	John Bethin for Maddock's tenement ; Edward Ellis.
1730 Do.	Mr. Hugh Puleston for his lease tenement ; Daniel Johnson in Spakeman's tenement.
1731 Do.	Thomas Mulliner ; Thos. Bellis in Wm. Philip's tenement.

Ministers	*Churchwardens.*
1732 Robert Jones, Rector.	Thos. Jones ; Daniel Prichard.
1733 Do.	Mr. Thos. Hughes ; Thomas Moyle for "old Downward's" tenement.
1734 Do.	Thomas Randle ; Thos. Griffith.
1735 Do.	John Kerrison in John Earl's tenement; Samuel Randles for Llydiarty Gwint.
1736 Do.	Thos. Edwards ; Randle Bellis.
1737 Do.	Do.
1738 Do.	John Bradshaw in Griffith's ; Roger Richards in Young Clutton's.
1739 Do.	Richard Shone in Hanmer's ; John Peter for lease tenement in Wallington.
1740 Do.	John Dampart in Mr. Hollyman's tenement ; Samuel Randles for Gough's tenement.
1741 Do.	John Fisher for the Hill tenement ; Rogers Richards for Thomas's do.
1742 Do.	John Bellis in Morgan's tenement ; Joseph Newns for Caelicae do.
1743 Do.	William Parker in the Wern at the Bridge End ; John Hughes in Croft's tenement.
1744 to 1755 Richard Jones, Rector, John Ravenscroft, Curate, are the only ministers mentioned.	Philip Puleston.
1756 Robert Jones, Rector.	
1757 Do.	
1758 Do.	
1759 Do.	
1760 Do.	
1761 Do.	

Minister.

1762	Robert Jones, Rector.
1763	Do.
1764	Do.
1765	Do.
1766	Do.
1767	Do.
1768	Do.
1769	Do.
1770	Do.
1771	Do.
1772	Do.
1773	Do.
1774	Do.
1775	Do.
1776	Do.
1777	Do.
1778	Do.
1779	Do.
1780	Do.
1781	Do.
1782	Do.
1783	Do.
1784	Do.
1785	Do.
1786	Do.
1787	Do.
1788	Do.
1789	Do.
1790	Do.
1791	Do.
1792	Do.
1793	Do.
1794	Do.

Ministers.

1795	Robert Jones, Rector.	
1796	Do.	
1797	Do.	
1798	Do.	
1799	Do.	
1800	Philip Puleston, D.D., died 1801.	
1801	Rev. C. W. Ethelston.	
1802	Do.	
1803	Do.	
1804	Do.	
1805	Do.	
1806	Do.	
1807	Do.	
1808	Do.	
1809	Do.	
1810	Do.	
1811	Do.	
1812	Do.	
1813	Do.	Rev. Henry Santon, Curate.
1814	Do.	Do.
1815	Do.	Do.
1816	Do.	Rev. Thos. Turner.
1817	Do.	Do.
1818	Do.	Do.
1819	Do.	Do.
1820	Do.	Do.
1821	Do.	Do.
1822	Do.	Rev. George R. Downward.
1823	Do.	Do.
1824	Do.	Do.
1825	Do.	Do.
1826	Do.	Do.
1827	Do	Do.

Ministers.	*Churchwardens.*
1828 Rev.R.Fallowfield,Curate.	Henry Crane ; William Poyser.
1829 Do.	Do.
1830 Do.	Do.
1831 Rev. Hugh Matthie.	Do.
1832 Do.	Do.
1833 Do.	Do.
1834 Do.	John Davenport ; Philip Gregory.
1835 Do.	Do. to May.
1836 Do.	John Caldecott ; Jas. Maben.
1837 Do.	Henry Crane ; Charles Richards.
1838 Do.	Do.
1839 Do.	Do.
1840 Do.	Do.
1841 Do.	James Morris ; James Parry.
1842 Do.	Do.
1843 Do.	Do.
1844 C. W. Wynne Eyton, Rector ; Rev. J. W. Millman, Curate.	Edward Crane ; John Dawson.
1845 Do.	Do.
1846 Do.	Do.
1847 C. W. Wynne Eyton, Rector	Do.
1848 T. H. G. Puleston, Rector.	William Wilson ; Thomas Mullock.
1849 Do.	Do.
1850 Do.	Henry Crane ; John Sadler.
1851 Do.	George Richards ; James Clutton.
1852 Do.	Robert Davies ; John Nickson.
1853 Do.	Do.
1854 Do.	John Sandland ; George Lloyd.
1855 Do.	Do.
1856 Do.	James Parry ; Edward Crane.
1857 Do.	Do.

Ministers.	*Churchwardens.*

1858 T. H. G. Puleston, Rector ;

  Rev. J. Gale, Curate.   Thomas Edwards; Robert Lovel Taylor.

1859   Do.   Do.

1860   Do.   Robert Davies ; Thos. Caldecott.

1861 T. H. G. Puleston, Rector ;

  Rev. J. Lea, Curate.   Do.

1862   Do.   Job Parry ; Thomas Fearnall.

1863   Do.   Do.

1864   Do.   Charles Richards ; Wm. Bate.

1865   Do.   Do.

       (Edward Rogers, elected P. Clerk ; vice John Edwards).

1866 T. H. G. Puleston, Rector :

  Charles Bolden, Curate. Thos. Jones ; Thomas Cooke.

1867   Do.   Do.

1868 T. H. G. Puleston, Rector ;

  Hy. W. Trower, Curate. Thos. Jones ; John Cooke.

1869   Do.   Do.

1870   Do.   Thos. Jones ; Thomas Fearnall.

1871   Do.   Do.

1872   Do.   Thos. Jones ; Edward Edwards.

1873   Do.   Do.

1874   Do.   Thos. Jones ; Thomas Fearnall.

1875   Do.   Do.

1876   Do.   Do.

1877   Do.   Thos. Jones ; Levi Huxley.

1878   Do.   Levi Huxley ; Richard Huxley.

1879   Do.   Richard Huxley ; Joseph Piggott.

1880 T. H. G. Puleston, Rector ;

  Rev. G. F. Birch, Curate.   Do.

1881   Do.   Do.

1882   Do.   Richard Huxley ; Jonathan Houlbrooke.

1883   Do.   Jonathan Houlbrooke ; Thos. Jones.

Ministers.	*Churchwardens.*

1884 T. H. G. Puleston, Rector ;
     Rev.G.A.Irving,Curate. Jonathan Houlbrooke ; Thos. Jones.

1885   Do.   Do.

1886   Do.   Jonathan Houlbrooke; PeterRathbone.

1887   Do.   Peter Davies Rathbone ; Joshua Houlbrooke.

1888 T. H. G. Puleston, Rector ;
     Rev. F. B. Roberts,
     Curate.   Joshua Houlbrooke ; Levi Huxley.

1889   Do.   Levi Huxley ; Richard Huxley.

1890   Do.   Do.

1891   Do.   Jonathan Houlbrooke ; Hugh Fearnall.

1892   Do.   Joshua Houlbrooke ; Levi Huxley.

1893   Do.   Do.

1894 Rev. F.B. Roberts,Curate. Levi Huxley ; William Houlbrooke.

1895 Rev. T. Watson, Curate. William Houlbrooke ; G. Trevor Jones.

———

www.ingramcontent.com/pod-product-compliance
Lightning Source LLC
Chambersburg PA
CBHW030554040726

47497CB00008B/2720